STAR TREK
DEEP SPACE NINE®

THE
DOMINION WAR
BOOK TWO

CALL TO ARMS . . .

A Novelization by Diane Carey

POCKET BOOKS
New York   London   Toronto   Sydney   Tokyo   Singapore

This book is a work of fiction. Names, characters, places and incidents are products of the author's imagination or are used fictitiously. Any resemblance to actual events or locales or persons, living or dead, is entirely coincidental.

An *Original* Publication of POCKET BOOKS

POCKET BOOKS, a division of Simon & Schuster Inc.
1230 Avenue of the Americas, New York, NY 10020

STAR TREK is a Registered Trademark of Paramount Pictures.

A VIACOM COMPANY

This book is published by Pocket Books, a division of Simon & Schuster Inc., under exclusive license from Paramount Pictures.

ISBN: 0-671-02497-3

First Pocket Books printing November 1998

10 9 8 7 6 5 4 3 2

POCKET and colophon are registered trademarks of Simon & Schuster Inc.

Printed in the U.S.A.

One thing's for certain. We're losing the peace.

Benjamin Sisko

CALL TO ARMS . . .

CHAPTER
1

"SIR, THE STATION's shields are holding!"

"Impossible. Federation shields have always proven useless against our weapons. . . ."

Ah, battle and its surprises.

Damar's claim about the shields was unexpected, yes, but somehow the Vorta's response was a charming satisfaction. How good it felt to see the elegant "ally" confused.

In the cramped command area of this smelly Jem Hadar ship, Gul Dukat deliberately didn't look at the Vorta representative. So many complications—having to fly this breed of ship instead of a Cardassian fighter, crewed by the rocky, dim-witted Jem Hadar soldiers. The only familiar face, the only Cardassian face, was that of Damar, now manning the helm.

And having this Vorta individual on his flagship,

guiding the touchy alliance between the Cardassians and the race calling themselves the Dominion from halfway across the galaxy . . . little of this arrangement settled well in a man's stomach. This was a bittersweet situation, to have a Vorta on each Jem Hadar ship. At least they didn't insist upon also having a Vorta on each Cardassian ship. That would've been almost impossible to shove down the throats of Cardassian Guls.

He watched as asteroid-sized cauliflowers of flame and energy bounced from the shields of station Terok Nor as ships fired over and over. There was something satisfying about that, about the invading Jem Hadar vanguard finally feeling the sting of repellent force, giving Gul Dukat a surge of pleasure even as his own weapon fire sheeted ineffectually out into open space.

And seeing the Vorta's chiseled face and pale-jewel eyes crimped in confusion, seeing the self-greatened political officer of the Dominion set back a pace, was worth the momentary loss.

Dukat raised his chin—a childish but effective maneuver and gloated in the wake of the setback.

"I've found it wise," he began, "never to underestimate the Federation's technical skills or Captain Sisko's resourcefulness." Having blithely thus dismissed the Vorta, he turned to Damar. "Bring us around for another pass."

What a majestic sight—the chunky Cardassian architecture of Terok Nor, a clawed, leggy metal knot hanging in space, called *Deep Space Nine* by those who had occupied it for the past few years . . . the United Federation of Planets.

Soon the station would be Terok Nor once again, and there would be Cardassians running the powerful weapons, turning those arrays on Federation ships. That would be a good moment. Dukat had spent many years claiming that such a moment would come, and now it was imminent.

Yet, for just an instant, the order to open fire had come hard from his lips. Over these years he had formed a strange kind of relationship with many of these people, these enemies, upon whom now he would unleash the power of a spaceborne armada.

Hesitation? Regret?

Destructive energy burbled across the station's shields, and the shields held. The Federation had made some kind of adjustment. He had always appreciated the Federation for its ability to come awake and be aggressive, and now he had been given the little quirky gift of pointing out to the Vorta that the Federation could be tricky enough for good defense too.

At Dukat's order, an entire flank of the attacking armada had swung around for a second pass against the carefully directed returning fire from the station's upper phaser arrays. In his mind, Dukat could see Captain Benjamin Sisko and his crew working in the Operations center, doing nothing arbitrary, targeting every shot, for they knew they were alone out here. Other than their single battleship, the *Defiant*, now clearly visible beyond the station, there was no other support here.

Although that was a good signal that the Federation was spreading its defenses too thinly, Dukat knew it

also let Ben Sisko concentrate on only two fronts—
the ship and the station. That made the maneuvers
here simpler, and Sisko was good at punches in tight
quarters. The *Defiant* was right over there, setting up
the mine field that, when complete, would protect the
mouth of the wormhole which was the only portal for
Dominion reinforcements. The wormhole had to be
kept open, for the Dominion's sake, yet for Dukat
there was something nauseating about needing the
Dominion in order to take back Terok Nor. He longed
for ways to set himself and all Cardassians apart from
the Dominion, their musclebound Jem Hadar pawns,
and their silky Vorta mouthpieces.

All around them Jem Hadar ships wheeled in a
majestic dance and were obliterated into shimmering
blooms against the crisp blackness of space and the
encrusted metal body of the station itself. Still more
got through and continued attacking the station, and
another flank went after the *Defiant*. The station took
a hammering on those enhanced shields, but instead
of defending itself, the station's weapon arrays fired
upon the Dominion ships going after the *Defiant*. The
station was giving the *Defiant*'s crew cover, time to
finish that mine field.

A dangerous portent—Sisko apparently thought
that, between the station and the mine field, the
station was the more expendable. Arguable, but still
strange. . . .

Who was on the *Defiant*? Sisko himself? No, he
would stay with the station. Several of his officers—
Dax or Worf or Major Kira—could take command of

the ship, but Sisko would think himself more effective in running the station's defense grid and keeping track of all incoming attackers.

"Are you disappointed, Gul Dukat?" the Vorta asked him with that musically sickening voice.

Dukat's neck almost snapped off as he cut short a glance. He used the Vorta's name like a slapping hand. "Why should I be, Weyoun?"

"Perhaps this will be too easy. We will take the station today. Now that you've accepted the superiority of the Dominion, Cardassia will have what it could not possess on its own. Others too are seeing the great light of the Founders' wisdom . . . the Romulans, the Tholians, the Miradorn, and now even the Bajorans have accepted the inevitable and made treaties with us."

With a bitter smile, Dukat shook his head. "Do you actually believe the Bajorans wish to be our allies? No, no . . . and they're not afraid of us, either. Not those brats who fought me unremittingly during the Cardassian occupation of the planet. No, you misunderstand."

"Your instincts tell you differently?" Weyoun asked. "The Bajoran treaty is some kind of trick?"

"Not a trick . . . a message."

"From whom?"

"From Benjamin Sisko. He is their emissary with the beings who live in the wormhole. The Bajorans would listen to him. I'm sure he was the one who convinced them to make a treaty with the Dominion, just as I'm sure the treaty is a shield, not a bond. That agreement is a message from him to me. It means to tell me that he is already beginning to maneuver events."

Weyoun's intelligent eyes flickered with concern, then changed. "You read too much into things."

"Do I?" Dukat handed back. "Then I must be foolish to notice that Starfleet has not defended the station with a flank of ships. All we have here is the *Defiant,* which is doing a job over there, and the station taking the blows and defending itself. I must be overly cautious to appreciate the station's enhanced firepower and shields. No, there is some reason for this . . . perhaps they're sacrificing the station for some reason. Something else is at work here. . . . We would be imprudent to think else."

Around them, on every screen, Dominion ships speared toward the station. Several, at least eight, were instantly obliterated, lighting space with fireballs of primary detonation, then a second plume as the ships weapons or fuel ignited. Battle in space was a glossy thing. In a line with Dukat's flagship were the Cardassian flanks, which he had deliberately held back, allowing the Jem Hadar to take the brunt of the initial wave of defensive fire. Briefly, Dukat relished the foolishness of the ironheaded Jem Hadar and the arrogance of the Vorta, who had thought the vanguard was an honor and that Dukat was doing them a nice gesture by letting them go first.

The station's effort to defend itself and the *Defiant* was costing many Dominion ships, but anyone looking could see that the Dominion and Cardassian wings simply outnumbered the defenders and would overrun them eventually. Dukat also didn't care how many Dominion ships were sacrificed. They were hardly his comrades. Jem Hadar soldiers were manufactured minions who served somebody else. Their loss was no loss. Station weapons were now cutting into the Cardassian flanks too, but that was the cost of any enterprise, and the brunt had already been swallowed by Jem Hadar.

"Once again, your old control zone of Bajor will be yours, Dukat," the Vorta representative began. "You should be proud. You're returning in triumph."

"That may be or may not be," Dukat interrupted, tired of Weyoun's prancing. "Sisko is effectively blocking the wormhole, or he will have done so if the *Defiant* completes that mine field. Dominion reinforcements will be blocked from entering the Alpha Quadrant."

"His mine field will not be effective," Weyoun insisted. "We will simply detonate them."

Dukat looked at him—not just a glance. "We may detonate them until the planets fade around us. Do you see that monitor?"

"This?"

"No, the next one. That is a hardware configuration sensor. It's analyzing the mechanical construction of those mines. Do you see this small mechanism on each mine? This demarkation? That is a replicator housing. If we detonate a mine, those around it will replicate the mine until the field is complete again. We will waste time, waste energy, waste weapons—so at least for a time there will be no reinforcements. You see, we are not fighting peasants. We'll be dealt many more surprises before this is finished."

As cryptic as his words may have been, Dukat enjoyed lathering Weyoun with the sheer experience of a fighting past. Weyoun moved away—another benefit to a slight upper hand. Dukat deliberately moved in the other direction, to the other side of the helm where Damar was working. He lowered his voice and looked at the helm, hoping Weyoun would think he and the other Cardassian were discussing angle of approach.

"It's very important, Damar, that we take the station, not destroy it."

"The Dominion may have other preferences," Damar grumbled as his fingers nervously pecked at the helm.

"Weyoun and a handful of Jem Hadar stooges won't be enough to countermand my wishes about Terok Nor. We Cardassians are the ones who understand this sector and how best to control it. I want the station, Damar. It's important to me."

Damar looked at him. "You mean, it's important for you to take back the station you lost."

"It's important for me to be *seen* taking it back. Seen by the Bajorans, seen by the Federation and their new allies, the accursed Klingons . . . yes, that's what I mean. What do you think—is the *Defiant* finished laying the mines yet? Are they trying to decoy us?"

"They're not finished yet. If they finish the minefield and trigger the replication process, the wormhole will be useless."

"By all means, then," Dukat said halfheartedly, "we should stop them. Break off from the main flank and bear down upon the *Defiant*. Fire at will. And watch out for surprises."

A little vulturish light flickered in Damar's eyes. Steering the ship was gratifying enough under these crowded and challenging conditions, swinging and surging in and out of the station's claws, under hostile fire the whole time, while also avoiding an outright crash with any of the other dozens of ships, but to have a specific target was charming. Then the maneuver became a great game in which life itself and power were the prizes.

"Get them—" Weyoun appeared again at his side, watching the *Defiant* on one of the screens. "Get them quickly, Dukat! They're finishing the minefield—"

"Fire!" Dukat shouted, as much to break off Weyoun's chatter as to strike at the Federation ship.

Damar steered the ship, leading two other Jem Hadar vessels, in an attack strafe toward *Defiant*. The Federation ship had no choice but to veer away from its job of laying mines, driven by unremitting shots.

"Drive them away from the station, Damar!" Dukat called, then ordered the two other ships to break formation and bend around the *Defiant* to cut off any escape. To their left, the two other ships vied for the forward position, both edging ahead of the flagship.

"I want the lead!" Damar said as he leaned slightly.

"Then take it," Dukat blithely suggested.

But before Damar could gain speed and pass the other two vessels, space began to change in front of them. At the same level as the *Defiant,* just now passing that ship, space wobbled and shed like skin, revealing a Klingon bird-of-prey, acid green against the night, streaking directly toward them.

Weyoun's sylphlike manner dropped like a stone and he gasped.

"Klingons!"

CHAPTER
2

"EVASIVE!" Dukat called.

In the flanking position, unable yet to take over the forward strike, the flagship was able to angle aside, as was the ship on the far side. The ship in the middle, which Damar had so much wanted to best, took the brunt of full phasers from the Klingons and almost instantly folded upon itself and exploded. In a breath there were only two ships.

"Veer off!" Dukat shouted. "Veer off!"

"Fight him!" Weyoun insisted. "You are two! He is one!"

Dukat swung around, furious, yet somehow managed to keep his tone from flaring. "He is one fully armed bird-of-prey and we are two fighters with our shields down and our weapons half spent." Now he could shout again—"Damar, veer off!"

"The Klingon is pursuing!" one of the Jem Hadar crewmen called over his shoulder.

"He won't pursue," Dukat countered. "He'll protect the *Defiant*. Continue evasive. Rejoin the flank and continue attacking the station. I truly hate Klingons. . . ."

"Station's shields are at thirty-five percent," one of the Jem Hadar soldiers reported.

"Targeting weapons arrays and main reactor," the Jem Hadar gunner responded at almost the same time.

"Countermand that!" Dukat roared. "I want the station intact! Target shield generators! Keep hitting the same section until there's a break—never mind how many ships are destroyed! Don't bother filling those gaps! Attack wings and batteries, concentrate your fire on Section Seventeen of the outer docking ring. We have to penetrate their shields."

He continued barking orders. As long as he kept snapping this and that, the Jem Hadar soldiers stayed busy and there was no opening into which Weyoun could press a protest about leaving the *Defiant* to finish the mine field.

Everything was temporary, everything would change, and for now the station was the thing. And Dukat had a plan for that mine field.

As the flagship nursed its own wounds and bore down upon the station, a huge explosion erupted from the crusty gray surface of the docking ring.

"The station's main shield power is down!" the Jem Hadar engineer called.

"They'll switch to auxiliary," Weyoun anticipated.

"It won't hold for long." Dukat couldn't mask his feelings enough to ignore the sight of the *Defiant* setting the last few mines and turn on its rail, then swing away. As the ship left the screen, Dukat could clearly see the sprawling net of a thousand perfectly spaced replicating mines. All together, like a musical ensemble taking a single cue, the mine field flickered to a thousand tiny lights, then cloaked.

"Sir," Damar began, "the minefield—"

"I have eyes, Damar." Dukat cut him off, but Weyoun already noticed.

"This isn't turning out quite the way I had planned," the Vorta tightly said, his threat not very well veiled.

Dukat gritted his teeth. "A minor setback, Weyoun. . . . Once we take the station, we'll be able to dismantle the minefield without interference."

And take as long as I feel like taking.

Weyoun's voice became silky again, but the threat remained. "Let's both hope your confidence is justified."

Dukat started to turn, a permanent insult readying on his tongue, but once again he cuffed it aside and moved away from the Vorta, going instead to Damar's other side. "Damar, signal the reserves to prepare for final assault. Regroup the fleet."

"Another wave of our ships is entering Bajoran space," one of the Jem Hadar reported from over Dukat's shoulder.

"Look!" Damar pointed at the large screen which was focused upon the superstructure of the station. "They're evacuating!"

On the screen, taking advantage of the lull as the Dominion and Cardassian fleets stopped firing and regrouped, several ships of various configuration detached from the docking ring and streamed away from the station. Even the *Defiant* was now docked up, probably loading whatever it could carry and whomever was to serve aboard the Federation fighting ship.

"Evacuation. . . ."

Dukat watched for several moments. His station, his Cardassian jewel, would soon be his again. His. And this Vorta's. And the Dominion's.

"When I first took command of this post, all I wanted was to be somewhere else. Anywhere but here. But now, five years later, this station has become my home. And you've become my family. Leaving this place, leaving you, is one of the hardest things I've ever had to do."

Captain Ben Sisko stood rather stiffly before a random collection of personnel and citizens, at least those who were left, on the deep space station numbered "9" by the United Federation of Planets. The Starfleet people in the crowd were few and disturbed. They shifted and clasped their hands. Their eyes were downcast, at the deck. They were soon leaving the platform and the people they had protected for five years. The Bajoran citizens and other visitors and residents in the crowd stood still as clay, gazing upward at Sisko, remembering things much earlier than five years ago. They were being left behind, unprotected. Major Kira, Constable Odo, the barkeep

Quark, his brother Rom, their not so silent but constant customer Morn, various shopkeepers, Dabo girls, other Ferengi . . .

And still others, Starfleet and not, were watching him on screens all over the station. Probably his image, his words, were being broadcast all over Bajor as well. A planet in disappointment.

The last mine was set. The field was activated. Dominion reserves were moving in. The ugly announcement of evacuation had been made. All Starfleet personnel off the station. His command crew was dispersed to a variety of assignments—Dax would be on the *Defiant,* with him. Worf, now Dax's fiancé and the only Klingon in Sisko's command, had been assigned to General Martok and the Klingon bird-of-prey that had so boldly saved the *Defiant* and bought the extra time needed to set the mine field across the wormhole's mouth. Major Kira and Constable Odo would stay here, consigned once again to the oppression of the Cardassians, as they had been long before. Quark would stay to mind his business, and his brother Rom would stay with him, to run the business and be a spy for Starfleet, whatever good that would do here now. Nog, Rom's son, now a cadet in Starfleet, would go with Sisko and the *Defiant* as a member of the crew. There would be no cushion of training for him. He would be, like everyone else, plunged into real action.

All over the station, tender or desperate good-byes were being made, bargains of survivals, promises to live, to keep up hope, to struggle on. . . . Sisko's stomach suddenly knotted and he almost choked on a lump of rage. He squared his big shoulders, dealt with the sudden tension in this thick arms, and hoped the crowd would not notice the blush of fury rising in his cheeks, for that would give too much away.

"But this war isn't over yet. I want you to know while we were keeping the Dominion occupied, a combined Starfleet/Klingon task force crossed the border into Cardassia and destroyed the Dominion shipyards on Torros Three."

A few sparks of hope lit in the eyes of the crowd. Dax and Nog even seemed surprised and let it show. Sisko was gratified—by saving the news, he could give them one little gift before vacating the place he had sworn never to abandon.

Should he give them the details? Names, ships, images to which they might cling in the coming hard times? Should he describe how the Starfleet patrollers *Centaur* and *Majestic* had skirted all the sentry ships at Torros Three and stormed the shipyards without backup, trying to cover each other like two seed pods spinning in a light breeze?

No—these people needed their own victory stories. He had to give them time to make some before praising the actions of others when all these before him felt so helpless.

"Our sacrifice made that victory possible," he went on. "But no victory could make this moment any easier for me. And I promise . . . I will not rest until I stand with you again, here, in this place . . . where I belong."

Enough, enough—if he said more, something inside would snap. He buried raw frustration in a gesture, by tapping his combadge.

"Sisko to *Defiant*. One to beam aboard."

Blessedly, they were ready on the ship to beam him off the station right away. No ugly buffer of silent seconds. Controlling his expression, he watched the faces of the crowd distill into the lights and sparkles of the transporter beam. For a silly instant he wished it were they and not he being beamed away, but despite the illusion, his wish was only a wish.

He materialized in the transporter bay of the battle-ship *Defiant*, now his only home. Chief Engineer O'Brien and their personal Cardassian, Garak, were there to meet him, but neither said anything or dared to break his moment of misery.

He did that himself.

"Are we ready?" he asked.

"As soon as you give the word," O'Brien told him passively.

All an illusion—there was nothing passive about this moment and things would have to happen damned fast, but O'Brien was giving him time even though they didn't have any. In fact, O'Brien didn't even wait around for an answer. He rushed past Sisko and Garak, pausing only briefly at one of the engine stabilization controls before moving on to something else. Having not been on board in the past few hours, Sisko had little idea of what O'Brien was doing and this was no time to interrupt him.

"Mr. Garak," Sisko began, turning, and the rest of the question went unasked.

"I'd like to come along," Garak said instantly, "if

you don't mind. You never know when you might need a good tailor . . . and the simple fact is, I have nowhere else to go."

A good tailor. Tinker, tailor, soldier—spy. Garak's past was as simple as any crazy quilt. Sisko was somehow warmed. "Welcome aboard," he said.

"Dax to Sisko," the comm interrupted. *"The Dominion fleet is coming around for another attack."*

Well, here it was. O'Brien had given him a buffer, and Dax was giving him the rude awakening. All right.

"Release docking clamps," he ordered. "Prepare for departure."

Accepting a nod of encouragement from Garak, Sisko shook off depression's web and started acting like a soldier. He rushed to the ship's bridge and, to the apparent relief of his bridge crew, took the command deck. Did they think he wasn't going to show up? Maybe he'd need counseling for a couple of hours to get over this?

Not likely. But now wasn't the time to fight, either. The *Defiant* and Martok's bird-of-prey alone couldn't take on a hundred Dominion ships. Instead, *Defiant* and the Klingons dodged through the station's pylons, racking off enough shots at the attacking fleet to keep from being obliterated right away themselves. All they had to do was clear the station—

"Go to full impulse as soon as you can," he ordered. "We'll be back, but we have to get away first. Prepare to cloak!"

* * *

Major Kira Nerys and Security Chief Odo entered the Operations area of *Deep Space Nine*. The station, the *whole* massive structure, shook violently under enemy fire, wrecking the facade of elegance that Kira knew she wanted and suspected Odo wanted, too.

Odo left her side briefly and checked a readout. "The *Defiant*'s away," he said tersely.

"Signal the Dominion fleet," Kira responded. Oh, this tasted bad, bad, bad. "Tell them the Bajoran government welcomes them to *Deep Space Nine*."

Oh, sick! How many times over the past day had she rehearsed those words? Somehow she had forced herself to pretend they were just random sounds, like a combination to a door—except that this combination locked the door instead of unlocking it.

Odo stiffly said, "Message acknowledged."

"Good. That's the last message this station will be putting out for a while. Computer, initiate program Sisko one-nine-seven."

The computer dutifully said, *"Program initiated."*

A high-pitched electronic howl built up and screamed through the panels and trunks. Blue crackles of overload and discharge racked each station, frying the computer, monitors, and blowing out every system. A moment later, the plasma conduits stopped their usual pulsing and all the monitors snapped and went black. She and Odo stood together, watching everything they'd fought to protect blow up around them. Funny how your priorities could change.

Kira glanced around. "Dukat wanted the station back . . . he can have it."

Odo said nothing. He knew as well as she what this might mean—a slide backward to the days of labor camps and martial law under the Cardassians. But there were differences.

In those days long ago, Kira had been a scruffy, scrawny freedom fighter with a dirty face and a one-track mind. Odo had been a displaced alien using his shapeshifting abilities to change into silly things for the entertainment of others as a crippled effort to fit in. He hadn't even known in those days why he could do these tricks.

Now things were different. Kira was a major in the Bajoran military and had been adjutant to Starfleet's occupation of *Deep Space Nine,* a constant representative of the planet who had been privileged to command a Starfleet station and a Starfleet ship. It said something about Starfleet that they had so readily accepted her as an authority and treated her as if she had come through their own academy. The singleminded little girl who spent her life in the ditches of Bajor, defending only Bajorans, devoted only to Bajor, had over the past few years found herself accepted into and defending a much larger family.

Now the impossible was being asked of her. For the sake of long-sought quality of life on Bajor, she must shelve her revulsion at the return of the Cardassians and widen still more her envelope of toleration. No longer just a street urchin fighting behind smashed walls, she must help run the station even under Cardassian control. She must be the one to officially welcome them back. If only her intestines would cooperate.

As she and Odo walked the long Promenade together, not looking at each other, not speaking, Kira built herself up to doing what she must do. She hoped the station had wrecked itself enough that the Cardassians would have weeks of work ahead of them. As she and Odo approached the row of airlocks, Kira's eyes tightened, watching several Jem Hadar soldiers physically force open one of the hatches. Many more Jem Hadar, with their ugly pale faces like broken rocks, surged through and formed up ranks. A moment later she saw Dukat, his attendant Damar, and that nauseating Vorta step out onto the Promenade.

"This is a great victory for Cardassia," Damar's voice filtered down the long platform.

"And the Dominion," Dukat mentioned. His magnanimity was entirely fake, Kira knew, as was confirmed instantly by his glance toward Weyoun.

"Over fifty ships lost," the Vorta complained. "Our spacedocks on Torros Three destroyed—a victory perhaps, but a costly one."

"We'll discuss the repercussions later," Dukat said. "Right now, I intend to enjoy this moment."

Would you enjoy a pointy little fist in your nostril? Kira pressed her hands to her thighs as she and Odo—and Quark had joined them as they passed the bar—stopped before the Cardassians and that Vorta floater. This was it.

Uch.

"Gentlemen," she began, obviously forcing herself, "on behalf of the Bajoran government—"

Quark stuck his head between her and Odo, saying, "And the Promenade Merchants' Association—"

"I officially welcome you to *Deep Space Nine,*" Kira finished, annoyed that Quark had interrupted her slide down that slope.

Dukat tipped his head. "You mean Terok Nor. Don't you?"

Kira pressed her lips tight and pushed her tongue against her teeth. Did he want an honest answer? Did he want to hear what she *really* meant?

But Weyoun saved her from having to speak as he drifted forward to Odo, spread his hands, and gazed in obsequious adoration at the shapeshifter. "Founder . . . we are honored by your decision to remain with us."

Odo blistered and stiffened. "I'm not here as a Founder," his gravelly voice returned. "I'm the station's security chief."

Kira bit back a grin. She knew what that meant to Odo, and also how much of a lesser thing it must seem to Weyoun.

"Whatever you say," Weyoun allowed. "Nevertheless, having a . . . a *god* . . . walk among us is most gratifying."

"I agree," Dukat snapped, butchering the silliness. He all but slapped Odo on the shoulder—but luckily kept from doing that. "You, me, the major, together again . . . it should be most interesting. Now, if you'll excuse me, I'll be in the commander's office."

Dukat strode off, flanked by Damar and Weyoun,

swarmed from behind by their Jem Hadar stooges. Quark bugged his eyes meaningfully, shook his knobby head, and veered off toward his bar.

A moment later, Kira and Odo were standing alone on the Promenade, and the irritating part was over. The hard part . . . that was still to come.

Kira opened and closed her hands, then opened them again and tried to leave them that way. Might as well pry open clamshells.

"I don't know how he avoided rubbing it in," she muttered.

Odo watched the last Jem Hadar disappear down the curved corridor through the mist of smoke left-over from the ruptured vent main. "Rubbing what in?"

"He didn't say, 'my' office. I'd have expected that from Dukat. His sarcasm was always poorly veiled."

"Maybe he's changed," Odo huffed.

"Oh, yes," Kira said with a bitter twitch. "He's mellowed into a real sweetheart. Anybody can see that."

"Where do you think they're going now? To the captain's office?"

"Probably. They'll have to go through Ops. I wish I could be there when Dukat and that smarmy Weyoun see what they have to rebuild in order to use this station."

"Don't enjoy the dream too much, Major," Odo warned. "Dukat is a soldier. He'll be expecting the burnouts. He knows Captain Sisko would leave him with as crippled a station as possible."

"If not for that damned treaty Bajor signed, we

could've crippled it a lot more," Kira said through her teeth. "But I guess we have to be able to breathe if we're going to keep living here."

"Yes, we do. And we must bide time. Weyoun's first priority will be to dismantle the mine field so reinforcements can come through from the Gamma Quadrant. He'll have to let Dukat handle that. The Vorta are politicians, intermediaries . . . not soldiers."

Kira looked at him. "Are you suggesting that Dukat's priorities and the Vorta's may not be in line?"

"Would yours be, if you were Dukat? The Cardassians were once supreme here. Now they have formed a devil's deal with the Dominion. I'm sure no Cardassian is fool enough to think the Dominion will allow anyone to be its equal partner. I suspect Dukat views the arrangement as temporary, until his own ends can be met."

"What do you think Dukat wants?" Kira asked. "In the long run?"

"I don't know." Once again Odo gazed down the now-empty corridor. "But if I were you, Kira . . . I'd be watching him for clues."

"Our shipyards . . . destroyed!"

The Vorta's controlled features took on a ghoulish twist which gave Dukat definite satisfaction.

"Torros Three," he uttered, placidly looking over the report Damar had just handed him—even worse than the early reports. "The entire Dominion shipyard, decimated."

They stood now on the shattered remains of the Operations center, strangely resembling the condition of the station when Dukat had left it behind years ago. He too had destroyed everything he could before leaving.

He handed the padd back to Damar. "Acknowledge the information, Damar, but make no reports yet about the condition of the station. I'll handle that myself. Later."

"Yes, sir."

As Damar left, Weyoun watched Dukat. "Is this what you consider normal? To gain a station and lose a shipyard? Is this what Cardassians consider effective warfare?"

"We gained the station *because* we lost the shipyard," Dukat told him. "Or the other way around, depending upon your perspective."

"Do you mean to suggest that this was all some kind of Starfleet plan?"

"Oh, not exactly. I'm sure they have no pleasure in losing the station, but when that became inevitable I'm also sure they determined not to suffer a loss without a gain. The distraction allowed Starfleet ships to broach the lines and destroy Torros Three, yet they also managed to put up and activate that mine field. Though they lost the station and control of this sector, they did make us pay for the exchange. That is the nature of war, Weyoun . . . at least, it is on *this* side of the wormhole."

Weyoun leered at him, but regained control over his expression. "About that minefield . . . if they're self-replicating mines, what can we do to bring the network down?"

"They're not actually self-replicating," Dukat enjoyed pointing out. "When one is destroyed, its neighbors fill the gap. That's not 'self' replication—"

"I don't care what it is as long as you bring down the network."

"In time, Weyoun. I'm already working on it. Now . . . let me introduce you to the commander's office, Weyoun. This way."

Dukat nearly paused for a breath of success as the hatch doors parted and let him into the station commander's office. Once his, then Sisko's, and now his again.

He was fairly proud of himself and couldn't help but prance a bit. Though . . . not for taking back the station. The Dominion had helped too much for that. The Cardassians, after war with the Klingons, had been too weak to take back the station or any part of the quadrant from the Federation. Admittedly, they had to have help for that. The war had reduced Cardassia to an insignificant power, no matter what they wanted anyone else to believe.

When the Dominion came, the Cardassians had little power to resist and would've made thralls of Cardassia along with everyone else or been wiped out altogether. Instead, Dukat had maneuvered an alliance and made Cardassia useful to the Dominion. Many others had not been so clever and had been destroyed. That fate might still await others— the Federation, the Klingons—who could tell? But until then and probably after, Cardassia would survive.

And, of course, there was always a long-range plan. Everyone knew they were using each other. The Dominion, the Cardassians, the Bajorans, Tholians, so on. All knew there was no love between them, it was simply inconvenient for all to go to war right now when shorter goals could be realized. Dukat's long-range plan was that the Cardassians would eventually become so valuable to the Dominion that they would slowly become stronger. The day would come when the two forces would turn upon each other. Dukat intended that, on that day, the Cardassians would be strong enough to push the Dominion back through the wormhole and lock it there for good.

For now, Cardassia had to be useful and survive. In the short run, that mine field would stay there for a while. The longer the mine field was up, the longer the Dominion needed Dukat. He would make attempts to figure out the clever technology. That would take time. Dismantling them would take even longer. The tricky mines would baffle his engineers for as long as he needed them to be baffled. A few weeks to shore up the Cardassians presence here and Cardassian control. A few weeks to be seen in charge of things, to entrench himself and the Cardassian presence in the sector, to make Cardassia more useful, more necessary in the eyes of the Dominion. For now, that was Cardassia's only hope. For the future—hopes would broaden.

He needed time to patch up Cardassia's many factions. Dukat would have to iron away the wrinkles that had contributed to losing the war with the Klingons. Such a defeat must never happen again. Cardassia would not only have to be strong in ordnance and ability, but its power structure must be in line. Otherwise, there would be internal struggles and the foundation would crumble.

The Ops center was a smashed mess. The station had put up a monumental fight, and then the evacuating Starfleet contingent had taken an electrical sledgehammer to the main controls and every ancillary system aboard. The damage had veined through the body of the station, causing burnouts and overloads almost everywhere. Dukat had expected some damage, but not quite so much. Less disturbed than amused, he found himself admiring the work and wondered how to do it if that time ever came.

Not the most constructive of thoughts, but one had to be realistic.

Weyoun followed him into the office. "I assume Captain Sisko removed or destroyed everything of value?"

Dukat parted his lips to virtually confirm that assumption, but stopped suddenly as his eyes fell upon the nearly bare desk. Nearly . . .

"Not everything," he said.

He came around the desk and eased into the chair, but his settling there was blunted by a simple round element resting on the desk. A little white ball with red stitching, its white skin worn to a gloss. A bazeball, hadn't Sisko called it? He picked up the bazeball and turned it in his fingers.

Weyoun bent forward and looked at the worn palm-sized orb. "What is that?"

"A message." Dukat leaned back in the chair, bringing the dirty white ball with him. "From Sisko."

"I don't understand," the Vorta admitted.

"He's letting me know," Dukat said, "that he'll be back."

CHAPTER 3

"AH—THERE YOU ARE. I'd just about given up hope, Doctor. I would think that all those lunches we've shared would've entitled me to preferential treatment."

"Garak—"

Julian Bashir looked up from the analyses his workhorsing medical computer was choking out, and bridled his tone. All he could manage to do, though, was speak more quietly. The tension, unfortunately for a medical professional, remained in his voice.

"I've got twelve wounded officers and crewmen out there," he told their local Cardassian expatriate, who now stood in the clutter of medical supplies with a bruise glaring on his head like a billboard. "Each one is in a lot worse shape than you."

Garak's eyes flashed. "If you're trying to cheer me up, it's working. I feel better already."

The physician inside Bashir overcame the irritated human being outside. He reached up to probe Garak's forehead. After all, his job *was* to make people feel better.

Deep bruise . . . blunt blow. "What happened?" he asked.

"I was studying some star charts for Captain Sisko during the last assault when I had a sudden and somewhat violent encounter with a bulkhead."

Not entirely devoid of sympathy, since he'd been encountering a few bulkheads himself in the waves of battle, Bashir mentioned, "You'll live. . . ."

"I wish I shared your confidence."

At first Bashir ignored Garak's quip—Garak was always quipping, in fact Garak would go out of his way to pop off with lines when silence would do just fine—but something about this last declaration had a glint of not being a joke.

Seeing the doctor's expression, Garak explained, "Oh, I'm sure my head will heal, but the way this war is going . . . I wouldn't bet on any of us living to a ripe old age."

Bashir drew a breath of relief. He'd imagined some kind of Cardassian hit team coming after Garak to finally silence him, his strange and complex background in the secret Obsidian order, and his obvious collaboration with Starfleet. Any illusions that Garak was only a simple tailor had fermented into just an in-joke. Maybe not so "in." The fact that he had evacuated along with everyone else at *Deep Space Nine* proved that he wasn't living on the border and hoping to go back to Cardassia someday. Now he was deep inside Federation space without a particularly good reason, from the Cardassian point of view. So much for going home.

"I admit the odds aren't good," Bashir told him, "but they could be worse."

"Let me guess," Garak said around a wince as Bashir treated his abraded forehead, "you've used that genetically enhanced brain of yours to calculate our chances of survival."

Bristling again, Bashir's stomach knotted. He wished Garak would stop pointing out the tampered genetics that had boosted Bashir to higher intellect and even physical advantages of genetic engineering. Every reminder also echoed the haunting trouble of one Khan Noonian Singh for every Julian Bashir.

There just weren't that many nice things to say about it. Facts. Lots of facts.

"Calculating chances isn't that difficult," he muttered. "I simply began with a binomial risk distribution—"

"I'm really not interested, Doctor," Garak interrupted. "Ever since it became public knowledge that you were genetically engineered, you've used every opportunity to show off."

"I have nothing to hide anymore. I might as well use what I have."

Apparently even Garak—a man who had a past to hide himself—understood that. "Well? What are our chances? Over fifty percent?"

"Thirty-two point seven."

"I'm sorry I asked. . . . You're sure about that figure?"

"Do you want me to take you through the entire set of calculations?"

"Not really."

Then Garak muttered something, to which Bashir snapped, "Excuse me?"

"Look at you!" the Cardassian said. "You act like you haven't a care in the world. It's that kind of smug, superior attitude that makes people like you so unpopular."

Bashir withdrew his treatment of the wound. "Are you insulting me?"

"A thirty-two point seven percent chance of survival? I call that insulting!"

"Don't take it so personally. It's strictly a matter of mathematics."

"It's strictly a matter of our lives! You're not genetically engineered—you're a *Vulcan!*"

A grin tugged at Bashir's cracked lips. "If I'm a Vulcan, how do you explain my boyish smile?"

Garak's eyes caught that glitter again. "Not so boyish anymore. . . . Do you need help?"

"Help with what?"

"All your casualties out there?"

Somewhat warmed by the sudden change, Bashir looked at him. "Are you offering?"

"Well, I'm a tailor, aren't I? Garments, wounds . . . what's the difference, as long as you're sewing edges together?"

"There's a ghastly thought. . . . If you're serious,

I'd love some help. I have to get back to the bridge as soon as I can."

Garak picked up a sterilizer and began running it over his hands, to prepare for handling casualties. "Julian, how long do you think you can maintain this double duty? Being a doctor is enough in a war. Your skills are critical, not just to save lives, but to return crewmen to ships who desperately need them. Why do you feel you must also double as science officer for this one ship?"

"This isn't just *one* ship," Bashir corrected. "This is the *Defiant*. We're the only crew with extended experience fighting both the Cardassians and the Jem Hadar. The *Defiant* is the only ship that's taken damage from both enemies and has been shored up to stand against both types of assault. We're spread thin for technical service personnel. If I can be acting science officer as much as possible, someone else won't have to be pulled off a critical assignment and Dax is free to navigate and handle tactical. After all, Garak . . . you're doing double duty yourself."

"How's that?"

"You're a tailor. Now you're also a nurse."

"Oh . . . yes. Just call me Florence Nightingale. Where do you keep the needles?"

Three months of relentless fighting. Encounter upon encounter, skirmish upon battle, raid upon assault upon maneuver. A thousand cuts.

The *Defiant* slogged through space, between Martok's bird-of-prey *Rotarran* and a destroyer that was leaking plasma. On a lower plane, just visible on the main screen and the flickering diagnostic monitor to Ben Sisko's left, two other ships, including a Galaxy-class cruiser, were being towed, unable to muster their own motive power. All around them, like a giant rag doll torn into hundreds of pieces, floated what was left of the Second Fleet. Ship after ship, limping along, almost none without significant damage, sharing supplies, sacrificing equipment to keep each other going. The sight was sad and discouraging. There was no backup force to call upon, no extra support crew to replace those who had been lost. This was an all-out war, and everybody who could fight was already fighting.

There was no corner of the *Defiant* upon which he could rest his eyes without catching a thread of destruction. Around him, his crewmen were exhausted and gaunt. They'd given up trying to be clean weeks ago. Their faces and hands were smudged and sweat-smeared. The ship's life support systems had sacrificed comfortable temperatures for just keeping the air on board breathable—a real trick, considering all the leaks and contamination that nobody had time to repair because everybody was busy repairing more critical systems. Everything had to wait, so everything kept on breaking until it became critical. The squeakiest wheels were the only ones that got precious attention and rare parts.

The armada around them, once a beautiful sparkling spray of heavy cruisers, battleships, flank vessels, tenders, carriers, destroyers, border cutters, muscular support ships, fighters and Klingon birds-of-prey and heavy cranes, was now reduced to a third its original size. The ships that remained were bruised and stressed, suffering not only from the wear of battle but from simple starvation. Supply lines were growing thinner and weaker. Several starbases had been evacuated and no longer provided safe port or repair facilities. Almost every ship had gone to basic rationing. Personnel had been reduced in number and efficiency. There had been many casualties, most in the engineering and forward attack jobs—critical losses in posts that were not easily filled.

The situation was as grim as Valley Forge. Despite a few early punches, things hadn't gone well. For Sisko, it was getting to be a trial just to pretend that none of this bothered him. He'd made a game—or an exercise, perhaps—of seeming above it all, putting forth a tepid immunity to defeat after defeat, to insisting that just holding a line for a few days was a victory.

He sat in his command chair with no maneuver to command right now, except to watch as his crew monitored the position of several pendulum-shaped Jem Hadar heavy fighters, while those enemy ships decided whether or not to pursue the maimed Starfleet/Klingon armada.

To one side, Cadet Nog watched the monitors and tried to coax the ragged systems into reading accurately whatever they could pick up in space. On the other side of the bridge, Chief Miles O'Brien picked and patched at engineering systems that hadn't given a complete reading in two days. Jadzia Dax was at the helm, somehow appearing as unflappable as Sisko was trying to appear, but she pulled it off better. Despite a faded smudge on one cheekbone, she didn't even have a hair out of place. How did she do that?

Half the lights were out . . . the smudge might be just a shadow. Sisko couldn't tell and didn't really want to know. The cloying air of defeat was enough of a nemesis right now.

In his periphery, two significant lights came on, then winked off at the upper right of Nog's sensor controls.

"Cadet?" Sisko encouraged, forcing the young Ferengi crewman to have to tell him whatever he knew at the moment.

"Long range scanners show no sign of Jem Hadar ships," Nog answered nervously, as if he didn't believe what he was seeing. "Looks like they've broken off their pursuit."

Sisko had to admire the kid. Nog had managed to keep a sigh of relief out of his words.

O'Brien, on the other hand, made no pretense. His true feelings bubbled up like froth on Irish stew. "I guess they got tired of looking at our backs," the engineer grumbled. "Three months of bloody slaughter and what do we have to show for it? Not a damned thing . . . engage and retreat, engage and retreat. . . . Just one time I'd would've liked to see *their* backs—"

"That's enough, Chief," Sisko drawled.

But O'Brien wasn't done stewing, and they both knew Sisko couldn't really stop him if O'Brien wanted to keep talking. Luckily, all he said was, "Sorry, sir. Nothing a little sleep won't cure."

"We could all use some sleep," Dax said. "What's it been . . . seventy-eight hours?"

Nog turned in his seat. "Shouldn't we have heard something from the Seventh Fleet by now?"

Dax looked at him. Her voice mellowed them all. "I wouldn't worry just yet. The Tyra System is far enough away that it's going to take a day or two for any message to reach us."

"You think they can stop the Dominion?" Nog asked.

"You're damned right they can," O'Brien snapped. "Somebody has to."

Sisko sat back in his chair. Not exactly the Gettysburg Address going on in here. The good guys didn't always win, no matter what the legends said. Every force, even Starfleet, even the Klingons, eventually meets a more powerful force. That was the nature of life. Nobody was really at the top of the food chain. There was always somebody bigger, and even the biggest guys would eventually be brought down by a virus or a dog bite or just by time. Sisko was feeling very beatable right now, and singing songs of the valiant couldn't change a thing.

"Captain."

On the other hand, a three-month war wasn't that long, and it wasn't over yet.

"Captain?"

Sisko flinched, then managed to bury the flinch in a quick motion to scratch his leg. He looked at Dax. "Yes?"

"General Martok just beamed aboard."

"Martok? Why would he come aboard the *Defiant?* Has he got some news?"

"No." She smiled and stood up. "I think he wants lunch and he likes our mess hall better than his own."

"If he's trying to get me in a good mood," Sisko said, "I haven't been in one since I found out Jake decided to stay on *Deep Space Nine* instead of evacuating. No word from the station in over two months, no way to know if my son's still alive—"

"Relax, Benjamin. The Dominion wants their arrangement with the Bajorans to go smoothly for now. They won't kill the son of the Bajoran emissary."

"Or they might kill him on purpose, *because* he's the son of the emissary just to make a point of their superiority."

She took his arm and moved him toward the turbolift. "True, but I don't think Dukat would be casual enough to let that happen."

"Are you telling me you think Dukat would protect my son? Dax, you're hallucinating."

"I don't think he'd protect Jake for your sake or for Jake's. I certainly do think he would leave all his options open, and he knows you haven't abandoned *Deep Space Nine* willingly or permanently. I wouldn't make that assumption about you, and Dukat knows you well enough that he won't either. He'll want all the cards in his hand as long as possible. Jake is a pretty powerful card. I'm so mad at that kid for growing up—"

Dax laughed, lightening the whole ship somehow.

Together they strode the stuffy corridors to the

miserably dim mess hall. Martok wasn't there yet. In some ways, that was a relief. Time to sit down and pretend to have been there for a while. Time to put on an air of casual patience.

Dax took a table and Sisko veered off to the replicator for hot drinks. When he finally joined her, she was ready with a question as they clinked their mugs.

"So where do you think Starfleet's going to send us next?"

"I don't know," he responded with flat honesty. "But if I have any say in the matter, we'll be going right back to the front lines."

"Well said, Captain," a rough voice interrupted.

Sisko and Dax turned. At the entrance to the mess hall, General Martok's stocky but massive form took up almost the entire doorway. His craggy Klingon appearance was as welcome as springtime. Even cradling a freshly wounded arm whose bulky sleeve was bloodstained, ragged and filthy, Martok looked like a ray of sunshine to Sisko.

"And my ship will be at your side," Martok thundered on, flaring his one good eye.

Then he stepped aside to let a second Klingon, even more welcome, into the mess hall.

"Worf!" Dax rushed to the former Strategic Operations Officer of *Deep Space Nine,* enwrapping him with her willowy bear hug and jumped right up into his arms. He caught her as if she were a fluttering branch.

They made the oddest pair. . . .

Martok looked at Worf. "Tell her."

Dax twisted to look at the general, then back at Worf. "Tell me what?"

"It can wait," Worf protested.

"No, it cannot," Martok instantly said as he crossed to the replicator. "Raktajino," he ordered. "It has been weighing heavily on his mind."

"What it is, Worf?" Dax insisted. "What's wrong?"

Worf glared briefly at Martok. "It's about our wedding."

"You're getting cold feet?"

"You have scheduled the ritual sacrifice of the tar'g to occur *after* the wedding feast has been served."

Sisko drifted back in the chair and muffled a grin. Ah, somebody else's problems. It was as relaxing as the game of the week.

Dax stood back from her fiancé and accused, "We haven't seen each other in five weeks and *that's* the first thing you say to me?"

Standing his ground, Worf's normally severe expression became even more severe. After all, a man had certain principles to stand by, and the slaughter of the ritual beast at a Klingon wedding was right up there with honor, dignity, and the saving of the Federation from evil empires. Wasn't it?

"We agreed," he said, "it would be a *traditional* ceremony."

This from a Klingon who had lived about as untraditional a life as any ever had. And Dax wasn't torturing him on purpose or anything like that.

Dax shrugged. "Have it your way. First we'll shed blood, then we'll feast."

"As it should be," Worf nailed.

Martok swaggered to the table and rolled into a seat next to Sisko. "He has been unable to talk about anything else for days."

Smiling, Dax winked at Sisko. "He's such a worrier."

Sisko tried, but this time failed, to bury his smile at Worf's expense. Oh, well. Dax had probably set all this up anyway. She was hundreds of years old under that young-girl facade, had lived a dozen lifetimes and learned how to maneuver people.

How many times had she—or he, depending upon the case—been married?

One of these days, he'd have to ask.

"Take my advice, old man," Sisko said to her, "a small wedding is the way to go."

She grinned. "You get married the way you want, I'll get married the way I want." She took Worf's meaty arm and pulled. "I'll see you later, Benjamin."

He nodded. "Try not to break any bones. . . ."

As she and her embristled intended fled the mess, Martok slugged his raktajino and patted his injured arm. "Now that that's settled, I'd better go take care of this. Klingons make great warriors, but terrible doctors."

He started to get up, but the door parted and, as if summoned, their chief surgeon, Julian Bashir, entered. The moment might've borne a joke, except that Bashir was shaken and overwrought, thin and drawn.

"Captain—" he began.

General Martok presented his injured arm to the doctor. "Just the man I wanted to see."

Bashir ignored him, strode right past him, and

faced Sisko. His voice was strained, quiet. "We've been ordered to report to Starbase 375 for reassignment. . . ."

He paused. Sisko waited, but the doctor neither finished nor turned.

"Something else, Doctor?"

Drawing a breath, Bashir tried again. "There's news of the Seventh Fleet. . . ."

Sisko let a moment pass, then braced himself. "Go on."

Visibly battling between terror and rage, Bashir gathered his strength to make the report.

"Only fourteen ships made it back to our lines," he said.

The room seemed to shrink around them. Together, unshielded, they took the gut-punch information, then tried to struggle back. Sisko pressed a hand to his eyes.

"Fourteen!" Martok intoned. "Out of a hundred and twelve!"

The blow was irremediable. No Seventh Fleet. None. The concept . . . huge. Fourteen ships—survivors, not victors—couldn't possibly be called any kind of fighting force on this scale. Sisko could imagine the condition of those fourteen ships, and in that there was even less hope.

An entire fighting wing . . . a hundred and twelve ships . . . all those crewmen . . . all those irreplaceable captains and officers . . . gone?

Bashir's anger finally burst. His voice was husky, fierce, and he was bitterly frustrated. "Sir, we can't keep taking those losses! Not if we expect to win this!"

No fault in the venting. He was only giving voice to all the thoughts Sisko had been trying to keep in a box for all these weeks. Frustration with losses, frustration with Starfleet's inability to engage on this enormous scale. . . .

"Thank you, Doctor," he forced out. "That'll be all."

Perhaps embarrassed, or just exhausted, Bashir was unable to make any response or bow to protocol. He started to leave, then looked at Martok. "I'd better take a look at that arm."

With a final and rather cryptic glance at Sisko, Martok followed the doctor out.

Left with his ugly thoughts, Sisko stared over the top of his mug until his eyes ached and the skin around them began to twitch. He slammed the mug down, shattering the tabletop. Brutal defiance roared across his mind.

Something had to change. *Something!*

There had to be something more to do, some way to be more clever, some way to be *smarter* . . . there had to be something!

The door opened again and he almost lashed out, ready to punish some poor soul for interrupting his rage, but as he turned he realized he'd probably have lost his hand in the bargain.

Martok was back.

"The doctor can look at my arm later," the Klingon general said. "It is a time for us brilliant masters of strategy to talk to each other. Don't you think?"

Without waiting for an answer, he turned and

tapped a locking code into the mess hall entry panel. No one would interrupt them.

What did Martok have in mind that he didn't want anyone to interrupt?

The Klingon general was completely unintimidated by Sisko's undisguised rage. He picked up the toppled mug, said, "You didn't finish your raktajino. I'll get you more," and went to the replicator. "Sit down, Captain, and we'll discuss the weather."

CHAPTER
4

FEELING HIS KNEES CRACK, Sisko grasped the edge of a table and lowered himself into a seat. When Martok arrived with a fresh steaming mug, there was almost a human being sitting there.

"They knew," Sisko rumbled. "Somehow, they knew the fleet was coming and ambushed it."

"Of course they knew," Martok said. "The Dominion is run by the Founders. The Founders are shapeshifters. This table or my boot could be a disguised Founder. Your mug. That door. They could have spies everywhere. How can we keep a secret? How can the Federation and the Klingon Empire keep to ourselves information about the movements of entire battle wings? What can we do about it? Our enemies can disguise themselves as my hair if they want to."

"We have to stop it." Sisko's fingernails dug into his

46

palms. "What's going on at the admiralty? How can they possibly lose a hundred ships without retreating before it reaches that point?"

"They were ambushed, Captain."

"Even a retreat is smarter than that! What kind of orders are the captains being given by their flag admirals? Who lets things get to a point where a hundred captains and a hundred officer staffs and a hundred ships and all that hardware are utterly lost?"

He sat and fumed and steamed and stared. In the middle of the fume, a thread snapped.

"They know something!" he blurted, almost without thinking.

The Klingon tilted his head in question. "What?"

Shifting a couple of times, Sisko rolled his thoughts from side to side, then pressed a hand to the broken tabletop without even paying attention to the cut it gave him.

"Their victory was too overwhelming, Martok," he said. "Nobody can have a victory like that without knowing ahead of time what's about to happen. No one can take on a combined fleet and leave only fourteen ships! It's just *too* lucky! It's *too* lucky. . . . To me, that's a giveaway. In fact, it's downright foolish to use whatever information they had so brazenly. They've given away that they knew more than they should know."

Clutching any possibility, he stared through his fog of anger to the one little light.

Leaning forward, one elbow pressed to the table, he leered at the closed and locked door panel. "And I don't believe the Federation is littered with Founders.

There might be a few here and there disguised as side tables, but we've been careful too . . . we've had all sorts of countermeasures. Cooperative cells, isolation of factions, false information. . . . We've taken every precaution any sensible military body could be expected to take. And with false information, you'd think we'd have been able to track down at least a couple of spies, but we haven't flushed out so much as one. That doesn't—"

"Make sense," Martok agreed. "You're right. As soon as false information is acted upon, we know where the mole is. But not a boot or plate has come to life."

Sisko shook his head, fuming under every skin cell. "Because the Founders know what they can do, they think we expect them to do it, so they're either not doing it or doing much less of it than we imagine. We waste our time hunting boogeymen, and they exact win after win on a bigger scale. If I were the Founders, I'd be delighted with the Federation and the Klingons' being preoccupied with their ability to turn into a damned table lamp or chairs or carpeting. They know their talent would drive us crazy. They know half the population here is running around poking at inanimate objects and putting hot elements on tables and against walls and picture frames before they dare speak to each other."

A moment of tense silence settled between them, uneasy and filled with the clacking of desperate thoughts, but Sisko couldn't help feeling as if a vault inside his head had cracked and was leaking.

"We've been at peace too long," he uttered. "We keep on trying to defend ourselves into victory!"

"Defend?" Martok's one eye narrowed. "The fleet was on the attack when they were ambushed and slaughtered. How can you say they—"

"It was still a defensive mentality," Sisko insisted. "The Dominion attacked, then the combined fleet attacked back. I don't care how much of a front we put up, that's still defensive. It's not tricky enough. We *have* to come up with a plan to just outsmart the bullies time after time until we can become strong enough to push them out of our quadrant with a decisive win. That's going to take a long-range set of . . . ideas. And the guts to implement those ideas. And some way to contain the information so any spies are confounded. We can't be just a big committee and win this war. We have to get tricky, Martok. We have to start pressing our advantages."

"I see few advantages," Martok bluntly said. "The Dominion has been doing this for a long while. They have the Jem Hadar, soldiers whom they manufacture, with short life spans and nothing to live for but battle, so they might as well die battling. They are as expendable to the Dominion as the ends of our fingernails are to us. They're all programmed with the same information and the same personality. The Dominion can always make more—"

Sisko held up a finger. "Those might be advantages, General, if we use them properly. The Jem Hadar are manufactured, and have the same mentality, the same knowledge, virtually no experience, and no individuality. They're not clever. We should use cleverness against them. They're not experienced—we use experience against them. They're programmed—we use the advantage of individuality, spontaneity, and unpredictability against them. We haven't really been doing that. We've been fighting them based on *them*. We should fight them based on *us*."

Martok sat back and contemplated Sisko. The scouring look was clear—Sisko was being surveyed as either a desperate maniac or a distraught mid-rank officer who had snapped onto a whole new level of ruthless creativity.

Probably he wasn't very wrong on that. At first Sisko resented the glare, but after a minute realized he probably had snapped and that was probably good. He rolled the hot mug between his flattened palms and stared into the raktajino. For a few minutes there was silence as Martok let him simmer.

Then Sisko found his voice again and started talking.

"I have to get more control at Starfleet somehow," he said. "I have to get into the admirals' offices . . . get involved somehow with the strategic decisions."

"You're going to maneuver a promotion?" Martok pushed. "I would never take a promotion that would put me in an office with no ship under me. I thought you would never take such a thing either."

Sisko drilled him sharply. "No! No—General, I don't want any promotion! Not a permanent one, anyway. . . . Just something, some connection, something to wheedle me closer to decisions, give me some influence. . . . The strategies coming out of the admiralty have to be more creative, or we're just looking at more disasters. The admirals who we have now, they haven't fought this kind of a war. I've been out in deep space, defending the station, defending a planet, protecting a sector—you can't just go by the book on tactics! They don't understand. You *have* to be more creative. You have to change your thinking every single day, because that's what your enemy does. I've got to get close and start changing things."

"How will you do that?"

"I don't know yet. I don't know yet. . . . I'll do something though. . . ."

"No doubt you will. Take a sip while I stretch this arm before it seizes up more than it already has—ah!"

"How did you hurt your arm?"

"We were attacked by five Jem Hadar ships. I had three ships, but we vanquished them completely. All five destroyed, and I lost no ships and only forty-two men."

"Forty-two. . . . Where were you?"

"In the Argolis Cluster."

"Argolis? Why would . . . why were the Jem Hadar in a place like that?"

"To defend a moon and the old outpost upon it."

"Old?"

"A former Orion processing station. The Jem Hadar have turned it into a parts and repair bunker."

"Wait a minute," Sisko said, then hesitated. "A force that just had its source of reinforcements cut off sacrifices five fighters to defend a parts bunker? Are the Jem Hadar that much stupider than I've been giving them credit for?"

"They defended it ferociously," Martok confirmed. "We were able to take out five ships and lose none of our three. I was very proud. We picked up a faint emission and tracked it to this parts bunker. A minor repair facility. There are several set up in a grid across the Argolis area."

"Parts bunker. . . ."

"Yes. Forget about it, Captain. Not worth considering. I would never have fought had I not been surprised. Not for a prize of stone. It was completely automated."

"Automated!" Sisko planted his feet squarely and leaned forward again. "Are you telling me—Martok, are you trying to tell me that the Dominion sent *five* Jem Hadar fighters to guard *one* little facility that didn't even have any personnel on it?"

"Well . . . apparently. Here is my arm, after all—"

"These automated repair facilities . . . they were sending out some kind of emission that you tracked?"

"That was how we found them. A signaling or homing beacon for Jem Hadar ships who have been damaged and can't find the facility themse—"

Sisko slammed both fists on the table and almost stood up, then caught himself at the last moment and managed to stay in his seat. "Or . . . or . . . a grid of sensors!"

Squinting the eye, Martok didn't follow Sisko's line. "A grid? You mean that old string of outposts—"

Sisko drilled the Klingon with a penetrating glare. "Could it have been a sensor array? A grid set up to find the movements of ten, twenty, thirty . . . or a hundred ships? That would explain an emission!"

Martok sat still for a second, then another second, and a third. His voice rumbled in his throat without making words, then his single eye flared and he sat bolt upright. "Might that be it? Might they have dragged a string of sensors with them through the wormhole and set it up, disguising it and using it to look at us? They have never shown that kind of technology before—"

"We've never been in a war with them before! And all this time we missed the most obvious answer. They know what our ships are doing because they're watching us on a great big screen someplace!"

"If you're right, it must be more heavily guarded than even we saw. If they would sacrifice five whole fighters . . . " Already thinking of how to knock the thing out, Martok continued, "Such an array would pick up the movements of an attack squadron. We could never get close enough with any number of ships."

"A whole squadron, no, of course not," Sisko quickly agreed, "but could one or two ships get in? The warp signature might not be big enough to be picked up by a system-wide array.

"And we can't move in many ships without their seeing us coming through their own sensors," Sisko went on. "That means we'll have to distract them. Get them to pull ships off that sensor array, if that's what it is, and weaken their perimeter."

"How will you do that?"

"I don't know. There's got to be something they need . . . something they don't want destroyed that we *can* get to, or at least something we can threaten. I'll think of something, General. I will, or you will. We have to, because that mine field won't hold forever. Once it falls, we become a resistance movement and we could be doing that for the rest of our lives. I'll make a bargain with you, General. Somebody's got to save the Federation . . . and you're right, we don't dare share certain plans. We never know if we're talking to a disguised Founder, or if the desk is a Founder—"

"Are you saying we should keep this between ourselves?"

"Somebody has to do this."

"I agree, but . . ."

"If one of us is killed, then the other will bring in one more person of some power. Someone you can trust."

"Or you."

"Or me . . . but we've got to keep this in the smallest possible cells. If it gets out, it'll destroy everything. If we can make plans, keep it quiet . . . work with the authority we have, maybe get a little more . . ."

"We could, Captain, be working against the plans of others if we fail to consult with our higher commands."

"We'll have to take that risk. Why not? We're taking a million other risks. So we take one more. I'll get permission for the things that matter, but the long-range plan . . . if only I could act more freely, without reporting to so many people up the ladder. . . ."

"Captain Sisko, my friend, you are talking about maneuvers and actions which could lead to a court-martial for you."

A bitter smile broke across Sisko's face, so hard that he thought his cheeks would break. "What difference does it make, General? What career? This is bigger than careers. It falls to us. We have to be more ruthless. We have to go around and through and sideways and across our principles until we manage to do something the Dominion isn't expecting from us. We have to develop a plan to get back to DS9 before the mine field falls. That means the Federation and Klingon forces must be free to maneuver."

"Without being watched," Martok agreed. He took a long sip of his drink, thinking. "And I saw only the one outpost. We picked up at least four more signals."

Sisko nodded. "There must be at least eight, to do what I think it's doing. If it's a sensor array, it's certainly not going to be a bunch of big dishes that say 'You're being watched.' We'll have to determine what's part of the array and what's not. You take your ship—only one ship—and go check our theory. See if that's actually a sensor array and not an automated repair zone."

Martok raised his glass and clicked it on Sisko's. "I shall be gone in one hour. I will speak to no one but you about this. And while I fly back into the dragon's teeth, you, my friend, will be doing . . . what?"

* * *

"Captain? Captain Sisko, over here."

"Yes?"

"Vice-Admiral Warner will see you now. Come right this way. He's in the amphitheater with several other admirals and their staffs. They're reviewing the latest recordings and reports of maneuvers on the front—at least, what's left of the recordings. The admiral has agreed to meet you in the back of the theater. If you don't mind, please try to keep your voice down. Everybody's a little edgy lately."

"Oh, don't worry. I'll be quiet as a mouse."

"This way. Through this door. All right . . . shhh. This way . . . sitting right there, by himself. Vice-Admiral Warner."

"Thank you, Adjutant."

"You're welcome, sir. Just exit this way when you're ready."

"I will. . . . Admiral?"

"Oh—Ben. Um, sit down. Sit right down. I didn't know you were in the area. Not until a couple minutes ago, anyway. . . . Nice to see you."

"Thank you, but it may not be for long."

"Where's Dax? He's usually tied right to your lapel—or *she* is. . . . 'She,' right?"

"Yes, he's a she now."

"Weird, weird. . . ."

"You get used to it, Admiral."

"Better you than me."

"Zach, I'm going to come right to the point. I'll be very quiet, but I'm about to speak of something that'll make us both very uneasy."

"Mmm . . . well, I didn't expect this when I got up this morning, exactly. . . ."

"For nineteen years, we've never spoken openly of the incident at Theta Four-Z."

"I know. . . . And I always . . . appreciated that."

"It was a good silence to appreciate. You know, I didn't want command of DS9 when I was first assigned there."

"Out in the hind dusthole of space? Can't blame you there."

"I could've gotten out of it. One call to you would've done it. But I didn't contact you. I could've called in a few other markers, too, but I figured I'd just take promotion when it naturally came my way and not push. But I've changed my mind, Zach. You, me, right now . . . accept something. You've had a good career since Theta Four-Z. The event that almost happened would've ended your career. We both know you botched the mission. Accept it. If it hadn't been for me—"

"I know, Ben, I was there, remember? What are you doing this to me for? Why now, of all times? It's been laid to rest for nineteen years—"

"You owe me, Zach. Now you're in the admiralty. And I want something."

"God . . . I . . . Ben, didn't think you were this type. I thought I'd been right for once in my life. . . ."

"Too bad, Zach, you're wrong again."

"Okay, okay. . . . I just wish you'd done it at a better time."

"There's no better time."

"Shhh . . . shhh, please. . . ."

"Not only do you owe me, but we're losing. The admiralty is failing at what it wants to do. We're all going to die. They're going to destroy Earth. They're going to destroy Vulcan. If those two planets fall, everything falls. With Earth and Vulcan shattered, the Dominion can cut into every Federation anchor planet that tries to fight back. So you tell me, sir—what's your next idea? What're we going to do differently now that we've tried every established tactic in the book? We've tried brute strength, and got our backsides kicked, so that won't work. We don't even have the strength left to try that kind of thing again. It's time to change our ways. What's your staff's next idea? What's your adjutant's new brainstorm? What are we going to change?"

"Fine, Ben, let's say you're right. What makes you think you'd do any better?"

"How could I do any worse? We're defending ourselves to death, Admiral."

"Well . . . what d'you . . . what can we—"

"One thing I've learned out at DS9, if something doesn't work, stop doing it and do something else. Your people aren't doing it. Give me a chance. I'm calling in the marker, Zach. Put me somewhere. Give me an inside position."

"That's what you want? That's all?"

"That's all."

"You want a desk job? My God, you've got a ship! Do you know how many hotshot captains and first officers who've watched their captains die are badgering us for ship commands?"

"Don't give away command of the ship. I'll retain command for special missions. I just want the power to concentrate my own efforts and make use of a few contacts that nobody else has."

"What do you mean 'nobody else has'?"

"Nobody else has been running a Cardassian-built station on the border, guarding the only portal between two quadrants. If there's another person like that in Starfleet, I'd like to meet him and see if he knows the secret handshake."

"Well . . ."

"If this doesn't work, you can court-martial me or shoot me. Then at least I wouldn't have to watch us lose."

"What do you want?"

"Anything. As long as it's near the admiralty."

"Who's flag are you under?"

"Admiral Ross."

"Well . . . uh . . . I can't reflag you. But . . . look, this is hardly a time for anyone to be seen using personal markers to advance themselves, so you've got to promise one thing. You absolutely have to keep this to yourself and keep my name out of it. It's got to be absolutely secret and just seem to go through the normal channels."

"I agree. And I fully expect that when this is over you'll demote me."

"Well, I can't promise that, fireball. I guess you'll just have to take your chances. Now, get out of here before somebody sees us together. Thank God it's dark in here."

Was there a man dismay'd?

CHAPTER
5

Permanent documentation file, Dukat, S.G.

The war continues to go well. Each day brings reports of new victories. It's only a matter of time before the Federation collapses and Earth becomes another conquered planet under Dominion rule. All in all, it's a good time for Cardassia. And . . . the Dominion.

GUL DUKAT strode out of his office and gazed over the Ops center, manned now by Cardassians and Jem Hadar troops. The place looked much more normal to Dukat, with the grayish faces of Cardassians and the chalky exoskeletal Jem Hadar rather than the soft, plain multihued faces of Terrans and Bajorans. This was much better. More secure. Tidier. Quieter.

And it was making him very nervous. Things, yes,

had been going well, rather too well. The Federation had put up a massive resistence since the taking of *Deep Space Nine,* but since then things had tapered off to a series of bluntly controlled actions which neither gained nor lost much for either side, and that was, in Dukat's mind, suspicious. Even now, after two months, he felt the constant presence of Ben Sisko, as if the air were painted with the captain's face. The baze—baseball . . . Dukat had actually tried several times to muster the will to throw the thing away, but there was something cloying about it, something that kept him from becoming too complacent, and he knew in his soldier's mind that that little ball was doing him a great service. These people from Earth, in particular, were bewildering. Unlike the Klingons, the Vulcans, the Cardassians, and the Dominion, the people from Earth seemed to have no particular strengths, no special talents, little unity of purpose or thought or opinion, yet they seemed continually to be the axis of history.

Strange and disturbing, those people.

Dukat ambled down the steps, nodding silent laud to his officers and crew, shining in the adoration of the Cardassians who saw this post as so vindicating, pretending that the stone-faced Jem Hadar, who had no expressions at all, were adoring him too.

Oh, here was Damar, his adjutant now. Damar still seemed uneasy, but that was Damar's general condition and Dukat was growing used to it. Damar was only happy in the midst of actual assault when he was distracted from worry by action.

"I have new reports on Federation ship movements

and one new supply line," Damar reported. "The station's sub-processors are almost repaired, but the conduit trunks in Ops and several of them in ancillary stations are still suffering feedback and burnout. We have insufficient parts to repair everything at once, so we are—"

"Prioritizing. I'll leave it to you, Damar."

They strode out of Ops and through the station to the Promenade, where stiff-lipped merchants were keeping up the best appearances even though the Cardassians didn't want to buy anything and the Jem Hadar never needed anything. Several people nodded to Dukat, who forced a winning grin and returned their gesture. Wonderful day, wonderful station, wonderful everything.

"How is the mine field today, Damar?" Dukat asked, then enjoyed Damar's teeth-gnashing at the mention of this sore subject.

"Slow," Damar said. "The replicators are proving more stubborn than we expected."

"Don't worry, Damar. In time the mine field will fall. Until then, we are supreme here and becoming more and more supreme by the day."

"You seem complacent, sir," Damar rather boldly told him, the culmination of several days of frustration. "If the mine field doesn't come down soon, Dominion forces will be too depleted to maintain control. The Federation and the Klingons will be able to make more effective strikes and we will hesitate to strike back for fear of losing too many ships to keep control—"

"Patience. Patience, Damar, patience. . . ."

"Sir, I don't understand the way you're running this outpost!"

"Keep your voice down. Pleasantry and cooperation, after all, and contentment and order."

"Sir . . . contentment . . . this kind of approach . . . confuses me."

"You only understand force, Damar, but there are other ways to our ends."

Damar twisted as they walked, to glower at him. "What *are* our ends? To hold the sector for the Dominion? To be pawns no better than the Jem Hadar? Is this our end?"

Slowing his pace to keep from arriving at the wardroom too soon, Dukat lowered his voice. "We have an end, Damar, we Cardassians, but things must happen at a certain pace and I must control the pace."

Damar's eye twitched. "You must?"

"Yes. I must eventually be the undisputed commander of Cardassia and all our forces."

Halting in mid-step, Damar puzzled and stared. "You want . . . more than the sector?"

"Oh, yes, much more," Dukat admitted. Speaking of his plans was a risk, but he needed Damar on his side if his orders were to go unquestioned.

"Damar, compose yourself and listen to me. We both know that this cooperation between Cardassia and the Dominion is uneasy. The Dominion is strong right now and we are weakened. Our arrangement with them bolsters us for now and puts us back in some authority, but the Dominion retains the senior position, as our everpresent Weyoun is prone to daily remind us. Once the quadrant is under Dominion control, what do you think will happen to Cardassia?"

A moment of silence slid between them. Clearly Damar had not thought of this.

"In its present condition," Dukat went on, "Cardassia would collapse, would it not?"

"Why would it?"

"Because the moment we tried to resist the Dominion on our own power, a dozen factions would rise in Cardassia and struggle for control. We'll never get the chance to organize and fight the Dominion. We'll bring ourselves down with our own confusion."

He paused, turned, and gazed out over the miniature civilization of *Deep Space Nine* and its current denizens.

"I never wanted to be a despot, Damar, yet that's what I was forced to become when I ran Bajor and the station all those years ago. . . . It was the Bajorans themselves who forced me to behave in despicable ways. They kept resisting, you see, even after I tried to give them ways to cooperate. I would tell them a hundred Bajorans would be killed if they killed ten Cardassians. They'd kill anyway, and force me to keep my promises. What else could I do? They kept upping the ante, no matter how much I tried to get them to sit back, relax, and accept Cardassian presence. I did what I told them would be done, and they got angry. Isn't that odd? If they had just accepted Cardassian control and a certain amount of tribute and strictness, they could have gone about their lives in relative peace. They're the ones who forced the terrible conditions. Discipline had to be maintained. I kept trying to explain, kept giving them options, and they continued to take the most difficult paths. . . . They resisted, I had to get tough, they resisted more, I had to get tougher. . . . Just when I was getting close to control, the ruling council of Cardassia decided Bajor wasn't 'worth' keeping."

Damar didn't join him or come to his side, but spoke from behind. "I remember. . . . It was humiliating to leave."

Waving a casual hand, though he didn't turn, Dukat tossed off, "Oh, I never let it show . . . but, yes, I was haunted by an entire race of people laughing at Cardassians . . . laughing at me . . . like children who play a prank on an adult and spend hours laughing at the dullwitted adult. Sooner or later the adult has to teach them the correct order of things."

"Yes, sir . . . returning is a great vindication for you," Damar allowed, but the enthusiasm of his words was not communicated in his tone. Dukat suspected Damar thought he should say that, whether he believed it or not.

"It is," Dukat responded. "However, there must be much more. A carefully crafted series of events and changes for Cardassia . . . specific and subtle rebuilding of our abilities, cautious but definite reorganization of our command structure . . . a thousand little things and dozens of big ones. . . . The Dominion, you see, Damar, needs us now. We're expedient for them, but any Cardassian who tells himself they will need us ultimately is living a dream. They don't know the

Alpha Quadrant well, and there's no point fighting a multi-front war. To them, we Cardassians are little more than a convenience. They don't have to construct us as they do the Jem Hadar and the Vorta—you notice they didn't put brains and bulk in the same packages. . . . No, Cardassia will never be friends with the Dominion. Right now we have a common enemy, and that . . . *that* is Cardassia's only chance. If we try to take on the Dominion now, we'll crumble. In time, and with the proper focus, we can rebuild, get more technology, more strength, worm our way in . . ."

Perhaps the silence from behind him now implied that Damar thought he had gone insane with his new position. Dukat didn't care. He was no longer thinking about Damar or even about the station whose populated core he now gazed down upon. Never before had he known instinctively and intellectually that his reach could be so wide, his ideas so critical, his plans so reverberating. He balanced in his hands the future of Cardassia as would be dictated by cleverness, patience, caution, and the taking of opportunities that would bubble to the surface.

"The Dominion isn't as strong as they pretend to be," he murmured on, "or they wouldn't need us at all. Bringing everything through the wormhole to fight a war is an enormous undertaking. Millions of people, thousands of ships, facilities to maintain the ships and people, ketracel white to keep the Jem Hadar alive—this is not easy, this undertaking, and despite Weyoun's kneebending, the Founders are *not* gods. Cardassia may have been militarily defeated by the

Klingons, but we have something the Dominion does not. We are *here*. We have things here which the Dominion doesn't. We have a planet. We have outposts and colonies, establishments, factories, and billions of people. No matter how brilliant and strong the Founders may be, if they're going to run a war, they need hardware and a place to park their fleet. They need a friendly port on this side of the wormhole. As long as the mine field stays up, they will need Cardassia."

"Are you saying," Damar tenuously began, "that we must collude to keep the mine field up?"

"Oh, no, we'll be pressured to bring it down eventually, but we will stall and in that time do other things toward our ultimate ends. We will let the Dominion have control, but not too much control. They will have victories, but not victories too overwhelming. In the meantime, they will help rebuild Cardassia. In parallel, I will maneuver controlling interest of the great Cardassian machine. All factions must be aligned by then. When the time comes that we need once again to be strong, we will already be strong. If the Dominion utterly conquers the quadrant, a mighty and consolidated Cardassia will be a power to reckon with. If the quadrant rises and throws off the Dominion, likewise we will be the strongest power here, not the weakest. I must be relentless in my pursuit of the smallest chances that bubble to the surface in the coming weeks. I must balance Weyoun on one hand and our own council and citizens on the other, always putting forth an image of singleness with the Dominion, while also maintaining our own identity and value. Cardassia must not collapse again, Damar, and for that . . . I must exact finesse."

Ben Sisko had twitched himself to threads waiting for Martok's coded contact, and after a while had instructed his private computer to relay a message to his combadge, despite the innate danger of being overheard, and had taken to walking the halls of the *Defiant* and the starbase. Since the ship was docked up, one in a long line of ships waiting for repairs, he could stride freely from the comfortable confinement of the ship to the broader, brighter corridors of the starbase. His hand flinched every few seconds, resisting the urge to tap the combadge and demand to know whether the computer were on the ball and listening for Martok.

He completely ignored all the other people hurrying past him, having gotten used to the idea that he'd been gone for years and hardly anybody here knew him, ignoring them so completely that he'd stopped even meeting people's eyes and nodding a hello. He just padded along from area to area, pretending to be going somewhere, keeping his eyes pretty much on the carpet.

So when someone passed him, then paused and turned, he didn't even notice.

"Sisko? Ben?"

Combadge!

No—it was this person who had just gone by.

Sisko retrieved his hand from almost hitting the button on his chest, and turned. There stood a vaguely familiar face—human, pale complexion, regulation-trimmed full beard, blond as dandelions, Nordic nose and . . .

"Charlie? Charlie!"

Forgetting his troubles for a blessed moment, Sisko met the other man in the middle of the corridor between a stinky lab and a noisy power chamber.

"Charlie Reynolds, I haven't seen you—don't tell me! Ten . . . fifteen years?"

"Twelve," Reynolds told him. "My third daughter had just been born."

"Lucy!" Sisko leveled a finger at his old lab partner's face.

"Lindsey," Reynolds laughed. "Not bad . . . not a bad memory at all."

"How many kids do you have now?"

"Eight! Five boys, three girls! Had four more boys after Lindsey."

"And you, the Bachelor Hound of Barrack Four!"

"Yeah, well, every hound settles down for the right milkbone. My wife's fifty pounds heavier and ten times prettier than when I married her. She's the greatest mother you ever saw, Ben, just takes to it like wind through a tree. She still wants more kids. You remember Magdalena, right?"

"Short hair, round face, eyes disappeared when she smiled."

"They sure do! Man, I forgot how tall you are."

"I forgot how blond *you* are," Sisko retaliated. In a surge of reverie he pinched Reynolds' combed beard. "What is this? You look like a faded picture of my grandfather!"

Reynolds laughed. "Yeah, well, you still look like

my uncle's shadow. Look, I heard about DS9. Must've been awful to leave. I know we're not supposed to feel like these places and ships are 'ours,' y'know, but . . . can't help it."

"Right, we can't help it," Sisko murmured sentimentally. "How's that horse's behind you call a ship?"

"Oh, look, don't forget that a centaur is human where it counts. Brains!"

They laughed together and turned to stride arm in arm away from the noise and stink of the workaday corridor.

"What're you doing here?" Sisko asked him.

"We evacuated Blue Rocket. Didn't you hear?"

"Oh . . . Charlie . . . no, I hadn't heard about that. I remember reading the reports when that installation was set up. Must be . . ."

"Ten and a half years. I shuttled the settlers out there myself. Brought in all the supplies, helped put the buildings together, took my family out there. . . . We were going to start over. My wife's mother's buried there and two of our kids were born right in the first hotel. We were really proud and, damn, were we happy. Last week I finished pulling the last civilian out. Nothing left now but a lot of half-harvested mills and the prosthetic plant. I wouldn't even have left the bastards the buildings if it'd been up to me, but the settlement council, y'know, they've got these hopes of going home again."

Sisko nodded in empathy, and more than a little guilt. For the first time he realized he wasn't the only one that had left behind the place he called home, that he and his friends and their station weren't the only evacuation, the only sad defeat, the only reassignment.

Reassignment—it sounded so cold, and in fact it was meant to be. Far better that soldiers not get too attached to a place they were assigned, a place they were essentially guarding, a place that was temporary, but somehow it never turned out that way. When a man invested his skin and blood and toil and risk into a place, into neighbors and hopes, responsibilities, change and growth . . . it wasn't simple anymore. Like him, Charlie Reynolds wasn't just a captain doing a job, following orders. He was one of a pattern of people who had staked everything on their own resolve and Starfleet's ability to protect the quadrant.

Feeling like an idiot for his self-pity, Sisko asked, "Where are you assigned?"

"Cardassian border," Reynolds said. "We're doing infiltration for . . . can I tell you this off the record? Keep that toothy mouth shut?"

"Absolutely."

"We're scanning for Starfleet Intelligence. The *Centaur*'s crammed with special agents. We drop 'em off and evacuate 'em, doing recon all the way. We're cloaked most of the time, but lately we're having to sacrifice that as too energy-intensive. We're cloaking only very close to actual drop-off and reacquisition sites."

"Sounds like a grind," Sisko offered.

Reynolds' crisp blue eyes crinkled. "It wears you down. My crew's spread pretty thin, but we're getting used to that. I don't know, you kind of pace yourself and take one day at a time."

"I'm learning."

"Yeah, I bet you are. Listen, Ben, can we get together later? I'm on my way to something. The Cardassian border, to be sort of specific."

"The border. . . . Sure. . . . I'd like that. We can remind each other of all the goofs and gaffs back in aerial strategy simulation."

"You crashed a lot."

"Because you kept knocking my elbow trying to get your ship out of the way!"

The laughter lifted a hundred burdens. Purging, somehow, and Sisko felt as if this one small encounter were infusing him with a will to go on and a sudden patience. All things would come around in time, just as this chance encounter after fifteen years. Here they were, former lab partners from the Academy, assigned to the same starbase and flagged under the same admiral. Although he had left the place he thought of as home, he was somehow coming home here, too, and they all had a common purpose.

For the first time since evacuating the station, he felt as if he were not so alone. Unless Charlie Reynolds was a disguised shapeshifter, Sisko decided to feel better. Suddenly he wanted to be back with his crew, spreading the virus.

"Captain Sisko," his combadge suddenly bleeped. The computer! It was calling only his name, as programmed, with no additional information. No orders, no information.

As Reynolds furrowed his brow at the unusual call, Sisko tapped his combadge. "Sisko responding. I've got to go, too, Charlie. Let's not make this the last time we meet for another fifteen years."

"Twelve," Reynolds said with an impish grin.

As they separated toward opposite ends of the corridor, Sisko shook his head and laughed. "You just don't have that 'Captain' arrogance about you!"

"Oh, yeah, something you've mastered! I'll see you, Ben, all right?"

"You bet, you bet . . . the sooner the better. And keep that ship Derby-trim!"

"And the tail braided!"

CHAPTER
6

DUKAT LED THE WAY into the station's wardroom, with a rather stunned and blessedly silent Damar following him. Oh, well, so Damar was silent. So what? One thing Dukat definitely needed for now and for the future was Damar's silence. So much the better if he remained a little stunned and frightened by the wider picture.

Ah—Major Kira was here. Slim, quick, dark-eyed, teasingly boyish, always the dancing light of any party. And Weyoun . . . at least a cloying curtain in a corner of the party.

The first voice Dukat heard was Weyoun's milky delivery as the Vorta finished a sentence to Kira.

"—no idea how it pleases me to hear you say that."

Their entrance given away by the hissing of the door panel, Dukat lost his chance to overhear. Weyoun turned instantly and said, "Dukat! The major has just given me the most wonderful news. Bajorans are returning to the station."

"I'm well aware of that," Dukat said, depriving Weyoun of momentary superiority.

"Then I'm sure you share my delight in knowing that life here is returning to normal. The shops are reopening, the Promenade is abuzz with activity once again, and the Habitat Ring echoes with the laughter of happy children."

Too sickened by the sweet juice to look at Weyoun, Dukat looked instead at Damar, who offered a minimal shrug and told him, "I've doubled security patrols throughout the station." Then he crossed to the other side of the wardroom and looked out one of the ports.

Kira inhaled and held the breath. Apparently she didn't like that idea.

Weyoun noticed her reaction too and looked at Dukat. "Are such precautions really necessary?"

Dukat didn't want to respond, but there was no way out of it. "I've found that one can't be too careful when dealing with Bajorans."

"What's wrong, Dukat?" Kira spoke up. "Afraid we'll take the station away from you again?"

Damar pressed forward an inch. "You're welcome to *try.*"

Weyoun stepped between them before they got any closer. "Come now. There's no need for this petty bickering. We're all friends here."

"Are we?" the major pressed.

"Of course we are. And if you have a suggestion, Major, feel free to bring it to me at any time."

"Fine," she snapped. "We'd like the station's Bajoran security force reinstated."

Damar snarled, "I suppose you want us to give them back their weapons as well!"

"That's right."

"The station," Dukat interrupted, "no longer requires a Bajoran security force. Our troops can handle any trouble that arises."

Her eyes hot with resentment, Kira was especially enticing in her resistance as she swung back to Weyoun and claimed, "The Federation and Bajor always shared equal responsibility for station security. I *thought* you said we'd have the same arrangement with the Dominion. After all, we're all 'friends' here. Aren't we?"

Anxious, apparently, to preserve the treaty that kept Bajor in line with the Dominion—at least for now—Weyoun turned to Dukat and firmly said, "Perhaps you should reconsider your decision."

Too much. Dukat's inner alarms, even the ones of his insult meter, started ringing.

"The order stands," he said. "You may trust the Bajorans, but I don't. And until they earn my trust, I prefer to keep them unarmed." Turning to Kira, he added, "And if you were in my position, Major, you'd do the same thing."

She didn't like it, but she did understand. Dukat could see that in her eyes, and hear it in her silence. The Bajoran bangle on her right ear swung back and forth as she raised her chin. Dukat's message had been clearly understood—this was no longer "always." Things were changed now and they would continue to change. He would walk the tenuously balanced beam between dealing with the Bajorans and letting them know they were inferior to the authority of Cardassians. He would only "share" so much.

Kira said nothing else to him, but started to leave. On her way out, Weyoun stepped to her side and said, "Perhaps it would be best to let the matter rest for a while. I'm sure, in time, all these minor problems will be resolved to our mutual satisfaction."

Stopping, Kira turned and told him, "I'll remember you said that."

"I'm sure you will. One last thing . . . Odo."

"What about him?"

"Is he aware that I'm doing all I can to strengthen the bond between the Dominion and the Bajoran people?"

Dukat listened carefully. Here was a strange twist to this arrangement—Odo, who was in Weyoun's perception a Founder, a god, was tightly aligned to the Bajorans and even to the Federation. Weyoun must indeed have his insides in a knot about that. He wanted the resident shapeshifter's approval, yet Odo would give it only grudgingly. Was that why Weyoun was so anxious to accommodate the Bajorans? Did he fear Odo?

"Why don't you ask him yourself?" Kira said, and Dukat almost answered, before realizing his thoughts had wandered and that she was still speaking to Weyoun.

"No—no," Weyoun resisted, almost whispering. "I wouldn't want to bother him. Good day, Major. . . ."

Quite plainly, Kira had had enough of Weyoun's pandering. She made no response to his pushed courtesy, but just exited as quickly as the space between her and the door allowed.

Dukat stepped closer to Weyoun. "Fascinating woman, isn't she?"

"I wouldn't know," the Vorta said. "But I do know we need her as an ally."

Damar's boots clunked on the floor as he approached them. "The Bajorans will never be our allies—"

"Out!" Weyoun barked suddenly. When Damar stopped abruptly and glanced at Dukat for support, the Vorta quickly said, "Don't look at him. *I'm* telling you to leave. Now!"

His thick face suddenly as chalky as a Jem Hadar's, Damar failed to mask his irritation. Among Cardassians it was customary for the adjutant to voice his concerns. Weyoun's strange authority as the Dominion's representative here made Damar's position questionable, and Damar didn't understand where he stood in this arrangement.

That alone kept him from pulling the Vorta's banana-shaped ears off and stuffing them down his mellow throat. Instead, taking a sturdy glance of support from Dukat, the adjutant drilled a silent threat at Weyoun, then simply left the chamber just as

Kira had, with the same cloud of smoke drifting behind.

"I find him useful," Dukat said before Weyoun had a chance to tell him to dismiss Damar for his insolence. He knew what was happening—Weyoun had lost the moment's attempt to define authority, so he pushed the point of Damar's having to leave. Dukat considered the slight to be a further win.

"In the future," Weyoun warned, "it might be prudent to include me in all decisions relating to station policy. Now, what about the wormhole? You assured me that you would dismantle the mine field within a month. That was *two* months ago."

"I admit that work is proceeding more slowly than expected," Dukat cannily told him, monitoring his tone carefully. "But these aren't ordinary mines. Every time we destroy or deactivate one of them, its neighbor replicates a new one."

"Self-replicating mines," Weyoun mused. "I'd like to meet the Federation engineer who came up with that. . . ."

"I'd like get my hands around his neck," Dukat offered, playing the game.

"We have to take down that mine field and reopen the wormhole."

"And we will . . . but there's no need to panic. We're winning the war."

"For the moment, yes. But to defeat the Federation, we're going to need reinforcements. And new supplies of ketracel white . . . soon."

"I said I'd deal with the mine field," Dukat claimed, "and I will."

Weyoun gazed at him in a piercing and plumbing manner. For a moment Dukat felt his insides crumple. Did Weyoun suspect his ulterior motives? The pressure of those milky alien eyes was undeniable. Dukat raised his chin a little and nearly leaned forward into the wind of Weyoun's silent accusation and the tides of suspicion. There was no evidence for what Weyoun might be thinking. Dukat had been careful to keep engineers working on the mines, but not the best engineers . . . not yet. Those working on the mines continually reported that the Federation devices were indeed tricky and clever, dangerous and quirkish.

And so they were. So they were.

"I hate them. I hate Dukat. I hate Weyoun. I hate myself."

"Calm, Major, calm. . . ."

"You be calm, Odo. The Vorta thinks you're a deity. You can at least be aloof around him and he pretty much leaves you alone. I hate the way he tries to make peace between Dukat and me when the last thing the Dominion really has in mind is peace. Certainly not peace with Bajor, anyway. They're just using us, and here we are letting them."

Kira had a drink in front of her but as yet hadn't taken a sip. Ordinarily she didn't like Quark's bar very much, but lately it seemed the only place where there was respite from the constant overlording of the Cardassians and Jem Hadar.

Oh, there were Cardassians in the bar, of course, clustered around tables, drinking and playing various games of chance, but they weren't as irritating in here as they were manning the station's controls or trying to pretend they liked having Kira and Odo around.

There were some Jem Hadar soldiers in here too, which was bizarre, since they neither ate nor drank, and they didn't seem to enjoy the tables. They just sat around and glared at what everybody else was doing, while their tubes of ketracel white bubbled placidly on their chests. All they needed was that stupid stuff. Why didn't they just go someplace else and suck on it?

She had her back to most of the bar, preferring the sounds to the sights of these current occupants. At least she could pretend they were somebody else.

Gazing at her from the seat on her left, Odo sat placidly, and of course since he was a shapeshifter he neither ate nor drank either, but somehow she knew he would like to. That helped. Unlike the hammer-headed Jem Hadar or the stubborn Cardassians, Odo would've been very happy to simply be one of the normal, living crowd.

"You should've seen Weyoun," Kira suffered on. "So sticky and obsequious. . . . The only reason he wants to get along with the Bajorans is because you're here, wearing that Bajoran uniform and he thinks he can get in good with you."

"Are you complaining?" Odo asked.

"No, no, I'm not complaining . . . exactly. I'm griping. I don't like getting what I want just because Weyoun's a prancing puppet. Eventually he'll get tired of that or the power structure'll shift, and then where will we be?"

"Of Dukat and Weyoun, who do you think has the most power?"

"I don't know. . . . Dukat didn't seem too intimidated, but he didn't push too hard either. I think Weyoun's getting annoyed that the mine field's still up and they can't get supplies or reinforcements, but I don't know how that plays for Dukat. Doesn't make him look very effective. . . . I don't know, really. I can't imagine what they think of each other. I'm telling you, Odo, Dukat has only one thing on his mind and that's revenge. He can't stand the thought that Bajor defeated Cardassia."

"You think he wants to re-open the labor camps?"

"Eventually."

"Then," Odo said, "I suppose we should be grateful he has Weyoun looking over his shoulder."

"Maybe. Weyoun's a hard one to figure out. I don't really trust him, but I do trust him more than Dukat."

She almost pinched herself. Did that make sense? Trust the devil she *didn't* know more than the devil she did? Went against all reason. . . .

Odo watched Quark as the Ferengi barkeep wandered through the crowd, grumbling at the Jem Hadar, making gestures of irony and frustration. "Weyoun knows that it's in the Dominion's best interest to honor its treaty with Bajor. They want to prove to the rest of the Alpha Quadrant they're true to their word."

Kira nodded in agreement, though they both knew that Weyoun's word and the Dominion's word only meant something as long as they needed it to mean something. "Weyoun asked me about you. He seemed very concerned about what you thought of him."

"I try *not* to think of him."

"He'd be hurt to hear you say that." Kira allowed herself a little grin. "I'll have to mention it to him."

The grin grew into a smile and the warmth of the moment gave them both some comfort.

Odo watched her musingly. "I'm glad you can still smile."

"Only when I'm with you," she admitted, knowing that might be a little dangerous given the way he felt about her—that and the agreement they had made in private to keep any burgeonings between them in the background until this struggle was won. Or lost.

"That's kind of you to say," Odo told her. He seemed genuinely warmed by the fact that she wasn't pushing him away entirely.

"It's true," she said, "When I talk to you, things don't seem as bad. Though every time I think of Dukat sitting in the captain's office . . . or the fact that the Federation seems to be losing this war and we're here doing nothing . . ."

Her bitterness, her anger, the sourness of having to swallow her rebel leanings and cooperate with the Cardassian presence—all bubbled out in her words. Kira felt her eyes sting as she looked around the bar at the Jem Hadar, the Cardassians, and Quark serving them.

She flinched—but it was only Odo putting his hand on her shoulder, a rare and welcome gesture of support.

"I share your frustration, Major," he said. "But right now, there's really nothing we can do except bide our time. It's like Captain Sisko said . . . Bajor must be kept out of the fighting."

Embarrassed by her flare, Kira forced her shoulders down. "And who am I to argue with the emissary?"

She smiled again, feeling a flush in her cheeks, and was about to say more when Quark approached and she stayed silent.

"Thank you for waiting," Quark said, casting a sour look back at his other clients as he deposited a tall drink in front of Kira. "Things have been a little busier than expected. This one's on the house."

After picking up the drink Kira glanced at the golden liquid, then looked up at him. "What do you want, Quark?"

"The usual. Peace, love, understanding, not to mention a generous profit margin, which I'm happy to say is looking more and more likely. You know, I never expected to say this, but as occupations go, this one's not so bad."

"I suppose that's true," Kira said, "if all you're worried about is your monthly balance sheet."

Quark surveyed his realm.

"I'm not just concerned about profit, Major," he said with a touch of candidness. "Look around. Do you see any ghetto fences dividing the Promenade? Or exhausted Bajoran slave laborers sprawled on the ground after a grueling day in the Ore Processing

Center? Do you hear the cries of starving children? I don't. Now don't get me wrong—I miss the Federation too. All I'm saying is . . . things could be a lot worse."

Leaving with that thought, he departed to take care of a paying customer who signaled him.

Kira didn't want to be left with that thought. Maybe that was part of the problem here. Things weren't bad enough.

"I hate to say it," Odo uttered, "but he's right. The Dominion seems determined to show it can be a friend to Bajor."

"If it's such a good friend, then how come there are no Bajoran security officers on the station?"

Odo let her troubled question fall into the muttering of the bar crowd. Kira couldn't blame him—they both knew the answer. The Dominion wasn't friends with Bajor. The Dominion was using Bajor. And the Romulans and the Cardassians, the Tholians and Miradorn—everyone who'd made a non-aggression treaty with them.

But maybe Quark was right. Maybe things could be worse.

Maybe.

"All right, General, what have you got?"

"Are you sure this is a secured channel?"

"Yes, and I'm relatively certain neither of my shoes is a spy. We have to move fast, before Starfleet suffers another big loss. The Federation might not be able to survive losing another hundred ships."

"Agreed. Your instincts were sound. The Argolis Cluster is peppered with sensor stations. They can watch the maneuvers of our fleets over many sectors with such a span. It must have been the source of their knowledge to ambush the Seventh Fleet so effectively."

"It's got to come down then. The array would see a squadron approaching, but might not pick up one assault ship."

"But the fighters guarding the array certainly would."

"Which means, General, that the fighters must be enticed away. We've got to create a diversion or a distraction, make trouble someplace else . . . hopefully real trouble, not just shadow trouble. . . . I wish I could talk to Dax or Worf about this. . . ."

"We made a pact, Captain. This would be between you and me. Times are difficult when we cannot trust the chairs we sit in."

"Don't worry, Martok, I'm not going to break the pact. I'll stick to our bargain. I'll come up with something to pull those fighters away from the sensor array. With the mine field in place at the wormhole, the Dominion is short of arms and they'll have to reassign those ships if something hot pops up in another area. After all, they think the array is disguised as repair depots. General, do something for me—pass this information along to Starfleet Intelligence and recommend it go to Admiral Ross. If it comes through me, it'll be too obvious."

"You want Ross to get this?"

"Yes. I need as much as possible of our plans to run through him, because then I'll have some control over suggestions and possible special maneuvers."

"I hope you have a warrior's luck, Captain, for this is a badly balanced bat'leth with which you fight."

"You're right about that, General, but what else can we do?"

"Most true . . . what else?"

CHAPTER
7

Starbase 375

"I'M GLAD YOU made it back in one piece, Ben."

"I was lucky. We lost a lot of good people."

"Yes, we did . . . and we're going to lose a lot more before this is over."

The office was small, gray, functional, and stark-staring empty except for the desk and chairs. On one wall was a large screen set with the United Federation of Planets great seal, a silver-rimmed circle with a starfield of major member systems, framed by a stylized leaf diadem. A couple of other static monitors, a small padd, and that was all. There was a left-over scent of cleaning fluids, very different from the scents of constant use Sisko was used to from DS9.

Admiral Ross was no older than Sisko, in fact he was a couple of years younger, but he already seemed tired and worn out. Sisko knew Ross had been a desk officer all his life, a good but uneventful administrator, had fit the role well, and somebody had to do it. As much as the cadets and the public relished grand stories of adventurous officers in the teeth of danger, anyone with sense realized that the firm platform from which those people jumped to their adventures was the administrative grid that kept the ships supplied, staffed, and effectively deployed. As an administrator of sorts himself for the past five years, an intermediary and an active duty officer with a hot desk to fly, Sisko had come to appreciate even more the so-called "desk jockey" admirals.

And he felt sorry for Ross, under whose flag the Seventh Fleet had flown.

The truth was heavy upon Ross as he spoke those words—many more losses would come and they both knew it. Keeping a confident face forward was getting harder by the day. At this rate, they'd be sending out kamikazes within a month.

"I hope you'll find this office satisfactory," Ross said.

Sisko fought to keep himself from reacting too much and made sure to appear bewildered. "I wasn't aware I'd be needing an office. I thought I was here for an assignment briefing."

"I'm afraid you're going to be here longer than you think, Captain," Ross said somberly. "As of right now, you're no longer in command of the *Defiant*."

Give him a little sense of shock. . . . Ask the right questions, but not too many. . . .

"Relieved?" Sisko responded with a measured note

of protest. "Have I done something wrong? I mean, other than losing a station at a critical location and negotiating a treaty between one of our allies and the attacking enemy?"

Ross smiled, and after a moment chuckled. "You've got the oddest sense of humor. . . . You and your people also figured out a way to effectively mine that wormhole and buy us time. You can't squiggle out of the fact that you did okay, given the circumstances. The station's still there, Bajor's not blasted to rubble—"

"Admiral, don't tell me how wonderful I am while you take away my ship."

"Sorry. I lost my adjutant, two vice-admirals, seven commodores, ninety yeomen, and thirty-one Starfleet Intelligence tacticians. I'm not saying it's permanent, but we need you available here at least part of the time, for a while."

"A while . . ."

"Just till we can rebuild the tactical core."

Sisko tried to cough up another protest, but couldn't read Ross well enough to know how far to push. Better not push at all. "What's my job?"

"You'll be my link to Starfleet Intelligence. I wasn't going to do this, but for some reason they suggested you specifically. Probably because you can help them figure out what to look for back in that sector you've been babysitting for the past five years. What the Dominion's weak points are, how to take advantage of those—you know more about Cardassian space than most of us, and that's where they've got their fleet and support systems staked out. See if you can conjure up some hits. Don't get me wrong, now, you'll be able to take the ship out on special missions, which you'll help develop. You won't be going out with the fleet, though. Would you mind breaking the news to your crew? I'll do it if you want—"

"No, sir, I'll do it."

"Okay. Sorry about this."

"Thank you, sir. You can be assured I'll get right to work. Sir, who's the SI contact for sectors Bravo and Echo in Cardassian space?"

"You don't waste time, do you?"

"We don't have it to waste, Admiral."

"That's why you're here."

"Oh . . . I know."

"Relieved of command? Why?"

"Admiral Ross didn't say. All he said was that we'd get our new assignment at sixteen hundred hours."

Sisko sat in his new chair, not looking at Dax as she paced his office and grilled him with a steady gaze that might see through him if he looked her in the eye.

"At least the crew's staying together," she sighed. "We *are* staying together . . . aren't we?"

"Count on it."

"So what do you plan on doing for the next couple of hours?"

Oh, the temptation to blurt what was on his mind!

But he'd made a pact with Martok—just the two of them.

"I hadn't given it much thought," he said. Instantly the irritation of lying to his oldest friend took a toll at his core. Keep the bigger goal in mind—

"Maybe this would be a good time to contact your father," Dax suggested.

"Maybe."

"Benjamin," she said, pressing her hands to his desk and leaning toward him, "you haven't spoken to him for months. Jake *is* his grandson."

How do I explain to him that I evacuated every Federation citizen off *Deep Space Nine* except his grandson?"

"You'll think of something. You always do."

"Grandson," Sisko mused. "The word brings up an image of a ten-year-old with a fishing pole or a baseball mitt. I still see Jake that way too . . . but he's not ten years old anymore. He's a grown man. Is it like this for all parents? Look at those long legs and broad shoulders, look him right in the eye after having to bend my neck for most of my life, but suddenly he's as tall and I am and telling me what he's going to do with his life? Is that normal?"

Dax smiled. "It's very normal, judging from every parent I've ever talked to. It's a big shock to realize you're not going to be the prime mover in your child's life anymore—*he* is."

"He is," Sisko echoed, "or the Dominion is. I wonder if he really knew what he was doing when he refused to get on one of the transports. . . . He wants to be a journalist, some kind of investigative reporter, and he thinks he has to be in a trench with bombs going off over his head. Who am I to say he's wrong? I veered off from my father's plans and ended up in the same trench. Why do I feel as if I abandoned him?"

"You're torturing yourself on purpose," Dax flatly said. "He stayed. It was his choice. Your father's going to be mad about it. Some things can't be changed. Deal with it, Benjamin, and don't let it eat at you. Everybody leaves the nest eventually. Everybody on that station and everybody on every ship is somebody's child . . . even Odo had parents I think."

"Quit making sense." Sisko shifted in his chair. "Get out of here while I call my father and get this over with. Go back to the ship and tell the crew about the command change."

"They won't like it."

"That's too bad."

"Right. See you at sixteen hundred."

"You did *what?*"

On the main screen, a steamy kitchen looked warm and welcoming, much more so that this cold, mold-pressed office. Whatever was bubbling on the stove in the background—Sisko could almost smell the aroma of one of his father's excellent concoctions. Joseph Sisko was famous in some circles for his soups and stews, a rather old-fashioned talent that had come around into favor again. Stuff that could be ladeled somehow melted the coldest core. At least one little corner of the quadrant wasn't on rations.

"Dad," Sisko attempted, fielding the glare of the gaunt dark face on the screen, "it's not quite as bad as it sounds."

Resentment for the patronization flared in his father's face. "You mean you *didn't* leave my grandson at the mercy of a vicious, bloodthirsty enemy?"

The little boy with the mitt in one hand and the fishing pole in the other made another quick appearance in Sisko's mind.

"Well, no . . . I did."

"Then it certainly *is* as bad as it sounds," his father reasonably accused.

"Look, Dad, it wasn't my decision," Sisko told him—pretty flimsy. "It was Jake's choice to stay behind—"

"Oh, so now you're going to blame this on Jake!"

"I'm not *blaming* Jake, but he's not a child anymore. He has to take responsibility for his own actions."

Should he bother explaining again—this would be the third time—that he hadn't known Jake was still on the station until it was too late? That Jake had certainly been given a half dozen opportunities to escape? That Sisko personally assigned Jake to a transport to make sure he had a place in the evacuation? Was it worth going over again or would he just be whining? His father wasn't stupid.

Joseph Sisko tried to be angry and unreasonable, but through this pause in their discussion something changed. The elder Sisko gazed over the light-years between himself and his son, looked over the edge of his disappointment that they couldn't be together, and made a clear effort to mellow his tone.

"You think he's all right?"

Ben Sisko ran through all the facts and theories in his mind—how the Dominion would treat the son of the Bajoran emissary, tolerate or antagonize him—no point cattailing himself again.

"I hope so. I'll get him back, Dad, I promise."

Ridiculous. What was he promising? To sacrifice his duties, his resources, his contacts, his markers, and everything else he could affect to change one situation which he probably couldn't affect? What kind of desperate idiot made that kind of promise?

"When?" Joseph Sisko shot back.

"I don't know," Sisko admitted. "It might be a while. I'm about to be given new orders and I don't know where they're going to send me."

Good—great. Twice in ten minutes he'd lied to two people he was close to.

"Tell them you want to go get your son," his father challenged.

"It's war time!" Sisko was forced to tell him. "It's not up to me. I go where I'm sent!" To get off that subject as fast as possible, he changed the subject and almost gave himself whiplash. "How's the restaurant doing?"

"All right," his father conceded. "It's been three weeks since I poisoned anybody. Are things really as bad as the news service claims?"

His father apparently wasn't going to be either fooled or misdirected.

"Maybe worse," Sisko admitted.

"You certainly know how to comfort a frightened old man."

The weight of deception grew heavier. "You didn't raise me to be a liar."

"I raised you to be a chef," his father shot back, "for all the good it did me. You know, there's something I just don't understand. You're always telling me that space is big, that it's an endless frontier, filled with infinite wonders."

"It's true—"

"Well, if that's the case, you'd think there would be more than enough room to allow people to leave each other alone."

"It just doesn't work that way. It should, but it doesn't."

For a moment, both men coveted a universe that didn't exist. They both knew perfectly well that a simplistic grade school approach of a complex galaxy just wasn't any kind of reality. The full tapestry of commerce, struggle, hopes, goals, efforts, and power shifts just couldn't fit into a nursery rhyme.

"I'd better be going," his father said. "The lunch crowd's coming in. You watch yourself, Ben, and bring me back my grandson."

"I will."

"I love you."

"Love you, too."

The comm clicked off, but only because Joseph

Sisko turned it off on his end. Well, that was done. Lies on top of lies, for as yet unseen goals. This was harder than Sisko had anticipated.

"Captain Sisko," the comm voice cracked from the deputy secretary's office.

"Yes?" Sisko answered.

"It's fifteen fifty-five. Admiral Ross, Commander Dax, and Dr. Bashir are here."

"Have them come right in. Why didn't you tell me they were waiting?"

"Sorry, sir."

The door opened and his two crewmen came in with Admiral Ross. Ross nodded a quick greeting, then went straight to the nearest wall monitor and shoved in a computer cartridge. "Here's the analysis of your information from Echo Sector, Ben. That was fast work on your part."

"Thank you, sir." Sisko came out from behind his desk and joined them at the monitor, exchanging brief glances from the perplexed Bashir and the ever-mellow Dax.

A stellar cartography map showed up on the screen, saving him from having to say anything to them or answer their silent questions.

"This is a great piece of information," Ross said. "Captain Sisko has isolated one of the Dominion's main supply depots for support of Jem Hadar troops."

"The *Defiant* is ready for a mission," Dax offered, anticipating the reason she had been summoned here.

"I know," Ross said, "but you won't be taking the *Defiant*."

Bashir scowled. "Then why are we here?"

"Captain Sisko had to be relieved of *Defiant*'s command. It's because, with all the requests for command status coming in to us, we couldn't justify giving one person command of two ships." The admiral paced across the star chart. "Starfleet Intelligence has discovered what we believe to be their main storage facility for ketracel white in the Alpha Quadrant, right here, deep within Cardassian space. We need to destroy it."

"Without the white to sustain them," Bashir offered, just thinking aloud, "the Jem Hadar won't be able to function."

"Without the white," Ross clarified, "the Jem Hadar will *die.*"

"I won't shed any tears," Dax said, "not if it helps win this war."

"It may be the only way we can end this war," Ross told her grimly, "other than surrendering."

Bashir, still lingering back, offered, "But how do you expect us to infiltrate Cardassian territory without the *Defiant* and its cloaking abilities?"

Sisko capped a grin that might've given him away. "I was wondering the same thing."

"You won't need a cloaking device," Ross said. "We have something even better."

He tapped a panel and the monitor changed to a live view of a Jem Hadar crab-shaped advance-attack ship hovering in a Starfleet docking bay. "It's the one you captured last year, Captain. Now you get a chance to see what it can do."

Julian Bashir turned to Sisko. "Do you even know how to fly that thing?"

"Not yet," Sisko told him. "But I intend to learn."

Sisko scheduled the mission for two weeks and would hear of no extensions. Still adjutant to Ross, he had managed to maneuver Ross into thinking that Sisko was the best operations commander for the ketracel raid, on the logic that nobody else would know about this. His own crew from *Defiant* would man the captured Jem Hadar attacker, further tightening the circle of knowledge about the mission, even though such secrecy required risking the life of Nog, a cadet. That was neither standard nor very wise operating procedure, but these were hard times. All support personnel from the *Defiant* had been isolated, then transferred to the attacker and had not been allowed to contact anybody since the move.

For two weeks Dax and O'Brien had been figuring out the systems and training the crew to run them. Not optimal, but it could be done in a pinch. Nobody on board would be an expert at everything, or anything, but individuals would understand a panel or two. The element of teamwork would be less available, but innovation might make up for it. The guidance matrix, thrusters, sensor fees, reactor core, induction, phaser coils, resonance emitters and the subspace grid had been made priorities—everything needed to make the ship go forward and fight if it had to. They just had to run the attacker, not run it particularly well.

The only major change was acceding to Bashir's request to install an infirmary and stock it with medical supplies and a limited-use diagnostic couch and sterile screen. Other than that, the Jem Hadar ship didn't even have a chair to sit in.

Sisko had refused requests to install anything else, even a food replicator. He didn't want any notable hardware changes that might be picked up on diagnostic sensors and give away the fact that any beings other than Jem Hadar were manning the attacker.

During these two weeks, as hard as it had been, Sisko deliberately didn't board the Jem Hadar ship very often or stay very long. If he were on board, the crew in training would turn to him with questions or for ideas, and he didn't want them to turn to him. He wanted them to figure things out on their own, because in the middle of action they couldn't be turning to him. Trial by fire didn't do any good if nobody got scorched.

On the fourteenth day, Sisko walked onto the bridge of the Jem Hadar ship, with DS9's favorite Cardassian shadow, Garak, tagging behind him, grinning like a clown at having been asked to come along. They were going into Cardassian space. Made sense to have a Cardassian face to offer up on a monitor if necessity dictated.

Nobody saw them enter. Garak remained a step behind him, and blessedly remained silent. For a few moments, Sisko simply stood at the lift vestibule and watched the crew whom he would soon be taking into the jaws of desperate danger. He watched, and listened.

"Guidance matrix, check," Dax was saying, standing rod-straight at the tactical controls. "Aft parabolic thrusters . . . check. Sensor feed . . . check. . . . Chief?"

At the engineering station, O'Brien was wrist deep in an open panel. "Reactor core . . . check. Induction stabilizers, check. Phaser coils . . . check."

"Nog?"

"Resonance emitters, check," the young Ferengi recruit chittered. He always sounded nervous. "Subspace field grid, check, signal processors, check—I think. . . ."

O'Brien looked up. "What do you mean, 'you think'? We've been training on this ship for two weeks."

The frustrated cadet glanced up. "I'd like to put a Jem Hadar soldier on the *Defiant* and see how well he does after two weeks. These controls are very . . . different. They take time to get used to."

Sisko smiled sadly, but still kept quiet, and gestured Garak to wait.

O'Brien picked at his board. "We don't have any more time. We're about to take this ship into enemy territory and we can't afford any slip-ups."

"I don't intend to make any, Chief."

"Good."

Nog shifted uneasily on his feet. "I still don't see why we couldn't install a few chairs on the bridge."

"Because the bridge wasn't designed for chairs," O'Brien told him drably.

"Well, my feet aren't designed to stand for long periods of time," Nog said. "They get tired."

"Then maybe we should leave you behind."

Suddenly even more nervous, Nog bent to his work. "My feet might like that, but I wouldn't."

"Believe me, Cadet," O'Brien drawled on, "it's not your feet that you need to worry about. It's your stomach. Maybe you haven't noticed, but there isn't a single food replicator aboard this ship."

"That shouldn't be a problem. Captain Sisko says we'll have plenty of rations."

O'Brien laughed. "Try eating nothing but field rations for three weeks, and then tell me it's not a problem!"

Dax looked around at them. "You want to know what *is* a problem? No viewscreen. Who builds a bridge without a window?"

Good point—Sisko glanced around, noting how closed-in the Jem Hadar command area really did feel. Even *Defiant*'s tightly packed bridge felt less like a box cave than this place.

He was about to speak up, notify them of his presence, when Julian Bashir appeared out of a back bay of the bridge and handed a padd to Dax. "The same people who build a ship without an infirmary. That's the list of all the medical supplies I brought on board. They're in my quarters, for lack of a better place."

Scanning the list superficially, Dax said, "We'll try

not to have any medical emergencies while you're asleep."

"I'm glad you find the lack of proper medical facilities amusing. But if trouble breaks out, it's not a viewscreen or a chair or even a sandwich you'll be wanting. It's a bio-bed with a surgical tissue regenerator."

Was there an edge to his voice? Sisko glanced at Garak, who was the doctor's friend, and felt as if the Cardassian were confirming his suspicion. Bashir had been notably colder, more blunt, and less easygoing since Dax and Worf announced they were getting married. Though it had seemed outwardly that he had long ago retired any hopes about himself and Dax, some things had a hard time dying a final death.

"Maybe," Dax flowed over the harshness, "but right now I'd settle for a viewscreen."

"Or a chair," Nog threw in.

And O'Brien—"Or a sandwich."

Sisko took a deliberate step forward, making sure that his movement was big enough to quell the banter. O'Brien saw him instantly and piped, "Captain's on the . . . I guess it's a bridge."

"All right, people," Sisko broadcast firmly, "prepare for departure."

Bashir, who would be manning the long-range sensor monitors—at least until there were casualties—asked, "Come to see us off, Garak?"

"Not quite," the Cardassian said.

"I've invited Mr. Garak to join us," Sisko told

them. "Considering we're going into Cardassian territory, he might prove useful."

With unshielded joy at his friend's presence, Bashir patted Garak on the shoulder as he stepped past him toward the long-range station.

Garak smiled at the welcome. "It's been known to happen."

From behind the picket-like stand of cylindrical monitor housings at the engineering station, O'Brien drawled, "Pull up a chair."

As Sisko crossed over to the command position, the lack of any place to sit down became irritatingly obvious when he had no command chair to slip into. He felt half undressed.

"We're cleared for departure, sir," Nog reported.

At the helm, Dax was watching him and waiting. He nodded to her. "Take us out, old man."

"Aye, Captain. Aft thrusters at one-half."

As the Jem Hadar prize pulled out from Starbase 375 and quickly left the star system behind, Sisko put on one of the virtual headsets with which the Jem Hadar crew operated their vessel. Creating a pinching sensation inside his head as its signal connected directly with his brain, the little screen immediately gave him a view of the stern of the ship and the beautiful construction of the starbase receding into the distance. When they cleared the last planet in the solar system, they were automatically clear of the Starbase-approach spacelane and were free to maneuver.

"Bring us about," he ordered.

The ship made a sudden and very harsh tilt, and the virtual-view of rushing space in front of Sisko's eye abruptly took a tumble. Judging from the wobbling of the crew, everybody else was having the same problem with equilibrium and recovery as Dax's hands shot across the helm and recouped her control.

"Just wanted to make sure everyone was awake," she claimed.

"We are now," Sisko said. "Let's keep it nice and easy, all right?"

"I can try. . . ."

"Set a course for the Cardassian border, heading zero-five-four mark zero-nine-three. Warp six."

"Yes, sir."

Starbase 375 was in a fairly well protected area, but also was one of the most distant starbases from Earth in this direction, putting them functionally much closer to Cardassian space than to the inner Federation sanctum. It took only a matter of hours at warp six to enter the patrol zone of the strongest fighting ships Starfleet had left and finally tease the Cardassian border, which in this area was not cleanly delineated. Many of the lines were in dispute. Sisko had no way to guess who might come popping up out of a cloud—Jem Hadar to welcome them "back," Cardassians who might be more savvy and demand to board, Starfleet who would probably open fire on an "escaping" enemy vessel, Klingons who might not care even to answer a hail before blasting away—anything could happen.

And something already had. His head was exploding.

He'd tried to deal with the headaches until the pain became so bad that he could scarcely see the view fed directly into his brain by the Jem Hadar virtual scanner headset. What good was this device if it gave him headaches so severe that he didn't care what it was showing him on its screen?

A hiss against his neck told him that Dr. Bashir had arrived with the hypospray to treat the headache, but Sisko didn't respond much. He was leaned over on one of the consoles, listening to the kettledrum in his skull. Not exactly jazz.

"There," Bashir said. "I wish I had more time to study the side effects of wearing that headset."

"Well," Sisko moaned, "at least we know one side effect . . . headaches."

"The headsets were designed to be worn by Vorta or Jem Hadar, not by humans."

"Captain," Garak interrupted, "may I make a suggestion?"

Keeping his eyes closed as the muscles in his neck began to unknot, Sisko moaned, "Only if you talk . . . softly."

"We saw Dukat wearing one of those headsets during the attack on *Deep Space Nine.* Perhaps Cardassian physiology is more compatible."

"Are you volunteering?"

"I suppose I am . . . the ship carries two of them. If I wear one, you won't have to. At least, not all the time."

"I agree with Garak, Captain," Bashir nearly whispered. "The less you wear it, the better."

Without moving much, Sisko picked up the other headset and passed it to Garak, who put it on.

"It's like having a viewscreen inside your brain," the Cardassian commented as he scanned the little vision being projected directly into his retina. Then he took a quick breath, seeming at first to be a reaction to the sense of reality he was experiencing, but an alert from Cadet Nog proved that more was going on.

"Sir, there's a Federation ship off our starboard bow, bearing one-five-seven mark zero-nine-five—it's the *U.S.S. Centaur!*"

Sisko almost put the headset back on, but hesitated. "That's Charlie Reynolds' ship—"

"I see it!" Garak gasped.

An instant later, a phaser blast rocked the ship, and they knew they were the enemy.

CHAPTER
8

ARMED, SHIELDED SHIP OR NOT, Starfleet phasers were still good.

Sisko put the evil headset back on. He had to see what was happening. Despite the twisting of his gut, he wasn't surprised at all. This was what he'd been afraid of from the moment Charlie Reynolds had said, "Cardassian border." Here was Sisko and his crew in an enemy ship, trying to execute a covert mission, unable to tell a damned soul about it without risking the security of the mission.

Luckily, Charlie didn't have a soul.

"Cadet! Open a channel to the *Centaur.*"

Sisko had let the Jem Hadar ship take a couple of hits before deciding to do that. It meant opening the circle a little wider and letting Charlie Reynolds and his crew know that this was a Starfleet covert operation. Might not be smart, but it was expedient. They had to go into Cardassian space with a ship that hadn't taken too much damage, or they might never get out again.

"I can't—" Nog's Ferengi face crumpled. "Our comm system's down!"

Good hit. Garak offered, "Then perhaps you should consider returning fire."

Bashir snapped him a glare. "We can't do that! They're Starfleet."

Another hit rocked across the deflectors, shuddering through the ship and almost knocking them off their feet. This standing up all the time was awkward.

"You tell them, not us," Garak warned.

Another hit—definitely war time, because nobody was taking any chances. Hit before you get hit.

"We'd better do something," O'Brien suggested, but made no specific claims to know what that something should be.

In a way the comm's being down was lucky. If they lived to get out of this—and they had to let themselves be killed before they would kill a Starfleet crew doing a good job—then the circle would remain tight.

"Dax," Sisko ordered, "get us across the border, maximum warp. Let's hope Charlie Reynolds knows better than to follow us into Dominion territory."

Reynolds—why did it have to be Charlie right after they'd just said hello after fifteen years? Twelve. Whatever. Reynolds had never been very clever but he was stupifyingly stubborn. He'd gotten through the Academy because he just never gave up, even though everything took him twice as long as it took most other captain candidates. Once he finally learned something, he never forgot it. He had limited knowledge, but his knowledge never faded like most people's. He knew his failings, knew his strengths, and dealt accordingly. And he was a genius at picking crewmen who made up for those failings. As a result, he had a deadly team over there.

But Sisko had a slight advantage—he knew who his opponent was. His former simulation partner. Unless Charlie had grown an improvisation muscle in the past twelve years, Sisko would still know Charlie's moves.

On the little painful screen in his head, a Starfleet patrol ship packed with special agents from Intelligence raced after them in hot pursuit, spitting fire. Ironic—working for Starfleet Intelligence, Charlie wasn't just protecting the border, but, like Sisko, was probably more worried about protecting his ship's secrecy. If he and Charlie knew about each other's tasks, they both had reason to keep their mouths shut. If only the comm system were working—

"How long before we cross the border?" he pestered.

Working furiously at the helm on evasive maneuvers, Dax gave him the cryptic answer. "We just did."

And the *Centaur* wasn't breaking pursuit. Reynolds was chasing them over the border. That confirmed Sisko's suspicion that Reynolds had authority to eradicate anyone who could spill the beans about *Centaur*'s presence.

"The *Centaur*'s still with us," Nog confirmed.

Sisko glowered. "Charlie never did know when to quit," he said halfheartedly, knowing he was under an obligation to keep mum about Reynolds' assignment, even to his own friends.

O'Brien reached to compensate for damage. "I hope he knows what he's doing. . . ."

"The question is," Garak reliably mentioned, "do we know what *we're* doing?"

The ship rocked and gulped under them as the Starfleet vessel hit them again.

"Captain," Dax reported, "that last hit damaged one of our guidance thrusters."

In that split second he reversed his logic. If he and his crew were killed, there would be no Jem Hadar capture with which to sneak into Cardassian space. Starfleet would lose its chance to destroy the ketracel white processing station. If the ketracel stores and the station that made more could be destroyed, the Jem Hadar would be on much more critical rations than anyone in the Federation and they didn't handle that very well. Suddenly the situation turned over like a pancake in Sisko's mind and the mission he and his crew were on became more important to the big picture than Charlie and his crew.

An ugly truth, but he accepted it in a moment. He would take his chances.

"Drop out of warp and come about." He turned to O'Brien. "Prepare to return fire."

Shocked and hesitant to fire on one of their own ships, the crew reacted with an exchange of disturbed glances.

"Yes, sir," O'Brien uttered.

Dax scanned her readouts. "The *Centaur*'s followed us out of warp."

Now at impulse, the two ships slipped past each other, exchanging fire, but it was easy to see that O'Brien's heart wasn't in the shots. He was hitting the *Centaur,* but only on the upper skin. No deathblows.

Even with the turn of events, the *Centaur* came about for another broadside and maneuvered for the superior position, above and just aft of Sisko. Dax managed to duck hard over and just briefly confuse the other ship.

"Target their weapons array," Sisko said, glancing at O'Brien. "Avoid their engines. I don't want to leave Charlie stranded on the wrong side of the border."

"We're coming about for another pass," Dax narrated, showing Sisko her intents.

"Charlie likes to swing for the fences," Sisko said, "so stay in tight. Attack pattern Omega."

In response, Dax maneuvered the Jem Hadar ship in a sharp turn to come in low, under the *Centaur* and O'Brien quickly strafed the other ship's underbelly as it flew by, scrubbing the sub-lateral weapons outlets. The *Centaur* made a wide banking turn back toward them as before, then suddenly changed its mind and angled away.

"The *Centaur*'s going to warp," Dax told them with a quiet victory overlying her relief. "It's heading back to Federation space."

"Yes!" Nog cheered.

Garak turned to O'Brien. "Nice work, Chief."

At the confirmation that he wasn't going to have to kill an old friend, relief poured over Sisko.

O'Brien didn't seem as comforted. "Thanks," the engineer said, "but I didn't know I'd scored a direct hit."

Sisko looked around for anyone who had an answer, because somebody would—

"Maybe you didn't," Dax spoke up. "I'm picking up three Jem Hadar ships headed this way."

Stepping to her helm and looking at the monitor, Sisko said, "Charlie must've seen them."

From one tension to another. . . . They watched as the three Jem Hadar ships streaked toward them, carrying enough combined firepower to turn an outpost to toast. Sisko braced for whatever might happen. Would they demand an inspection? Want a conversation?

The three ships roared in and sailed right past them.

Amazed, Nog said, "They went right past us."

Dax picked at her controls. "Without even bothering to say hello."

O'Brien scowled at his monitors. "They're too busy chasing the *Centaur*."

Gripped by concern, Bashir asked, "You think Reynolds will outrun them?"

Sisko drew a tight breath, but couldn't give them the answer they wanted. He couldn't give the order to turn and protect their comrades at the expense of their secret and their mission. Like them, Captain Reynolds was on his own.

"Charlie's been in tight spots before," he told them. "He'll make it."

What else could he say?

"I wish we could help," Dax murmured.

"We can't. Chief, get our comm system back on line. Dax, return to course. . . . Warp seven."

"They're opening fire! Targeting our engines."

"Engines?"

"Confirmed, engine target this time."

"Aft shields, quick! What took 'em so long? Get back over the border and we'll see what we can do. Continue evasive, Randy."

"Evasive, Charlie!"

"Don't shout."

"Okay."

"Chief, what's our engine status?"

Charlie Reynolds waited for an answer, and when nothing came he turned and squinted through the *Centaur*'s smoke-choked bridge at his chief engineer, who was bent over the console with half his body down inside a hatch-trunk. Unconscious?

Reynolds pushed out of the command chair, stepped to the rail, reached over it and caught the engineer's elbow. "Fitz, you all right?"

"Yeah, don't pull on my arm. I got a hot phasic adaptor in my hand."

"Thought you passed out."

"Not yet."

"How bad is it?"

"Pretty bad."

"Can we keep up warp speed?"

"We better."

"Don't suffocate in there."

"Yeah, yeah. . . ."

"Randy, go to warp six. Get us out of here. Roger, fire at will and keep it up. Don't let them get another engine shot or we're cooked."

"Warp six, aye."

"Firing at will, Charlie."

Reynolds stepped over the unconscious form of their tactical ensign and noted that the kid was at least breathing. He'd only been assigned yesterday. The only way to save him was to save everybody, and that meant the ship.

"Randy, warp seven if you can make it."

"I'll try." Helmsman Randall Lang brushed a hot spark off his sleeve and bent to his console. "Six point four . . . five . . ."

Reynolds reached forward from where he was standing next to the command chair and brushed a few more sparks off Lang's shoulder as a reassuring gesture that they were all still taking care of each other. Little things counted.

He liked his small ship and his small crew. Most of them had been together for more than five years, since the first major crew transfer to Blue Rocket. Nobody paid much attention, so nobody bothered to transfer anybody out of there. Blue Rocket had been a well-kept secret for most Starfleet people out there. Occasionally somebody wanted to leave and requested a transfer, but Starfleet almost never called with new orders for anybody. It was a nice, secure posting. Great for a guy with eight kids and a sense of neighborhood.

Till the war hit. Now, they were all out here on this limb, hoping to stay together. A few deaths, a few new recruits, but so far they were still mostly together. From day to day, though, they were nettled by a sense of impermanence.

He was their only anchor to getting back to Blue Rocket and reestablishing everything they'd given up. So far he'd managed to think, and to keep his crew thinking, that all this was just a temporary juncture.

To keep them distracted, to keep the ship relevant and necessary, to make sure nobody even thought of breaking them up, Charlie Reynolds had snapped at every chance for active duty. At the moment that meant infiltration. And *that* meant running hot before three Jem Hadar guard ships.

"One of 'em's veering off, Charlie." Science Officer Geraldine Ruddy had both hands on her console as she turned to him. "Vectoring back over the border."

"We're only worth two," Reynolds commented. "Keep tabs on that one till he's out of range, Gerrie. What're the other two doing?"

"Full speed, direct pursuit course. If we keep up this speed, they probably won't be able to get around us to ambush us."

Reynolds swung around to the navigator. "Any obstacles in our way?"

At the helm beside Lang, Roger Buick chewed on his perpetual toothpick and shook his head. "No, Charlie, we're full and by. Nothing but straight, straight, and more straight."

"Hear that, Rand?"

"I heard," Lang responded, his black hair plastered to his forehead, spiking over his eyes as he concentrated on his helm. "Throttle's up."

Prowling the command center, Reynolds churned with both curiosity and frustration. Why hadn't that first Jem Hadar ship opened fire on them right away? Why had a single Jem Hadar tried so hard to escape a single Starfleet cruiser that was in fact several metric tons smaller and notably less armed? They hadn't read any significant damage on that ship, so what was going on?

When that ship did fire, why did it only target the *Centaur*'s weapons array? Why were the shots so clumsy and halfhearted? Jem Hadar were predictable in their methods—full-out all the time, constant and untended aggression, shoot to kill. Why hadn't they done that?

"Maybe the ship was crewed by Cardassians," he murmured aloud, furrowing his blond brows. "Gerrie, did you get a scan on that ship?"

"Which one?"

"The first one. The one by itself on the other side of the border."

"The one we attacked?"

"Right."

"What kind of scan? Bio?"

"Yeah. Who was inside?"

"I didn't get that, Charlie. Their sensor shields were already up."

"If they didn't see us coming, why were their sensor shields up?"

"With the energy drain from that, I don't have any idea. You wouldn't run with it unless you had a reason, would you? I mean, would *they?*"

Reynolds shook his head. "They're ugly, but they're

not stupid. Something's going on. Where are those two ships now?"

"Same," Randy Lang said, "but still closing."

"Fitz, can we dump something to slow them down? Fitz!"

At his sharp call, the upper engineering trunk regurgitated Mohammed Fitzgerald, a handsome and perpetually young warp engineer with striking brown eyes and flaming red hair that was actually burned in a couple of places. Fitzgerald's face was pink with rushing blood and glazed with sweat. "You call me, Charlie?"

In spite of everything, Reynolds chuckled. "I think you burned your nose."

"I can't feel my nose."

"That's okay. If you get us out of this, I'll buy you a new one. You got anything we can dump on those two ships after us? Anything to slow them down, give us a couple of light-years? Coolant? Antimatter? Radiant—"

"Anything we could dump would cause us to have a corresponding slack in forward thrust," Fitzgerald said. "And it might also give us a surge off course, which would give them the edge instead of us. Why don't we just keep going straight and keep our aft shields doubled?"

As if in answer, a fierce hit from the Jem Hadar weapons struck the *Centaur* so hard in the port quarter that Reynolds was thrown bodily over the rail and Fitzgerald slammed backward to crash into the trunk he'd been trying to work in.

"Charlie!"

That was Randy Lang.

A hand gripped Reynold's arm and pulled him to his knees. He grasped the rail, then squeezed Lang's hand and said, "I'm fine. Drive the ship."

"Your head's bleeding."

"Drive, Rand, drive."

He tried to get to his feet, but he couldn't find them. He'd had them a minute ago. Oh—there's one.

The ship heaved again. Another hit?

"Captain's on the bridge, literally. Up you go." Fitzgerald hauled him to his feet.

All Reynolds had to do now was stay up. His head took a few seconds to clear. By the time he could think again, he was standing braced against the rail and the ship rumbling with another enemy strike.

"That was stronger. Are they getting closer?"

"One of them is," Gerrie Ruddy confirmed. "The other one's losing ground. We've still got a pit bull on us, though. We're well over the border, Charlie. They've got a lot of nerve to do this."

"The Jem Hadar don't care from nerve. They just go, go, go."

Lang glanced up from his helm. "You mean they'll just follow us until they catch us?"

"Or until somebody comes to head them off and help us."

"What if nobody comes?"

The cold answer needed no voicing, but Reynolds shrugged and blew it away with, "Then we'll crash land on Earth and take shore leave on Tobago, what else?"

To his relief, everybody laughed. Even the ensign on

the deck moaned and grinned up at him with an annoyed expression. Taking that as encouragement, Reynolds asked, "Fitz, you sure we can't make 'em skid?"

Fitzgerald turned a spanner over and over in his hands as he thought about that. "Well . . . you know, there's no reason we have to drop energy on them, is there?"

Reynolds dared take one hand off the rail as he turned to face Fitz. "Like what else? Something solid? Those cable bundles?"

He and Fitzgerald stood looking at each other for several seconds, as if memorizing each other's faces.

The engineer finally shrugged. "Why not?"

It was a fatalistic why not, but it gave them hope.

Bundles of cable meant for delivery to another ship, to be sent off someplace for some reason Reynolds didn't even know about, lay stacked in their durable and well-used hold. *Centaur* wasn't really a cargo ship or a fighter, but more Starfleet's idea of an all-purpose truck, used in the past for everything from transport to defense, mining to support, intelligence to the not-very-intelligent.

"You want to really mess things up?" Gerrie suggested. "Unspool the bundles before we jettison."

"Oh, what a great evil idea! Call below! Do it! Have the security team do it. Send some ensigns down there to help. Tell 'em to make it fast, not neat. Speaking of ensigns, somebody get that poor kid off the deck."

Since the navigating was done for this particular straight-line, Roger Buick stepped out from his seat, reached under the rail, and pulled Ensign Aryl from the upper deck through to the command deck and sat him on the edge of a step. "You hurt, kid?" Buick asked.

Reynolds kept one eye on them and one on the monitor showing the Jem Hadar pursuit ships as two gray dots dead astern.

"Of course he's hurt," he commented. He wanted to say something comforting and call the kid by his first name, but Aryl was Argelian and they only had one name.

"No, I'm not hurt," Aryl countered, which was just what Reynolds was going for. The kid pressed both hands to his face for a moment, rubbed some life back into his expression, pressed back his debris-dusted brown hair and pushed to his feet. "I can work, I'm not hurt. . . ."

"Next time you see a console explode, don't rush right over there. Take your post. Roger, you too."

"Aye, sir," Buick responded, and slid back behind the nav station, not that he had much to navigate. On a ship this small, he was their comm officer, too, but he also had nothing to comm. So he sat there and manned weapons they probably weren't going to expend unless they had to turn and fight.

Backing into his command chair, Reynolds tapped the comm. "Hold, tell me when you're ready with those spools."

"Almost ready. We've got about six of them unrolled. Four to go. They're just in piles, Charlie. That what you want?"

"That's it, Narhi. Make it good and messy. I want a big tangle."

"I think we can accommodate."

"Fast."

"Understood."

"And see if you . . . Rand, keep the speed up!"

"It won't—I'm losing power!" The helmsman hammered at his controls, then glanced fiercely at Fitzgerald. "Fitz, do something!"

Fitzgerald plunged for the part of the engineering console that was still blinking and jabbed at the panels, then looked around quickly. "Fall-off, Charlie! I can't stop it."

Reynolds swung back to the command chair. "Hold, it's now or never. Shove everything into the aft loading bay and jettison."

There was no response, but Reynolds resisted demanding one. He'd suddenly given them an order to get busy and he hoped that was what they were doing.

At the last moment he added, "Pitch the crates out, too, Narhi. And your tools."

Still no answer. Speed was slipping. The hits from the firing Jem Hadar pursuit ship now rocked *Centaur* every four or five seconds. Shields were flickering . . . the whole bridge lit like a holiday tree with alarm lights and electrical surges. Couldn't last much longer.

Geraldine Ruddy slammed a fist on her science console and watched the aft-view screen. "Jettison!"

CHAPTER
9

CHARLIE REYNOLDS rushed to Science Officer Ruddy's side, and was instantly joined by half the bridge crew. He glanced around ridiculously just to make sure that Randy Lang hadn't been lured from the helm or Fitz from the engines, but they were both watching one of Fitz's monitors, showing the same view of their aft space and the pursuit ship.

And then, all at once, a cloud of wire, cord, cable, spools, and parts of metal crates blew out into view and instantly hovered at the back of *Centaur* in a great wad.

"Get some speed, Fitz, anywhere you can," Reynolds said quickly. "We've got to outpace it!"

"I can tap the shields, but that's—"

"Do it!"

"Okay, increasing speed. Rand, take whatever you can get."

Lang sweated over his console, but his silent determination told them there was some thrust coming into his helm.

On the screen, the wad of tangled wire moved away from them and the distance between the Jem Hadar ship kept closing very swiftly. The enemy ship kept coming, then suddenly tried to veer off.

"Look!" Gerrie cried. "They've seen it!"

"Even if they miss it, we'll gain ground," Reynolds told them. Had to keep those spirits up.

But at the last instant the Jem Hadar ship's port wing caught just a hair of the floating tumbleweed. That was enough. The wad of wire and cable whipped instantly around and snagged the entire enemy ship, whirling in a sharp and slashing tornado. As it slammed into the ship's hull at fabulous velocity, it cut cleanly through several hull sections and halved the weapons and sensor arrays. Compromised in a dozen ways, the enemy ship whirled like a plate on a stick, round and round, gathering more and more wire and cable, and finally colliding with the pieces of metal crating. The metal smashed the ship surgically as well as any meteor shower.

Falling off from both speed and direction, the Jem Hadar ship heaved up vertically and started tumbling through space as if it were rolling down a rocky hill.

"Damn, what a great wreck! Rand, reduce speed. Conserve that power. Buick, call the Starfleet Sector Guard and tell 'em where to pick up another captured ship and a really embarrassed pack of jar-heads!"

The crew cheered, laughed, and rushed to their duties, clearly surprised that they'd survived at all, never mind made a capture.

Rather stunned himself, suddenly dizzy, Reynolds pressed a hand to his aching head and let his skull throb for a few seconds. Just letting it hurt somehow helped a little.

When his thoughts began to clear, he dropped into his command chair and opened his eyes. "Gerrie . . ."

"Yes?"

"Also put in a call to Starbase 375 as soon as we clear silence radius. I want an appointment."

"Who do you want an appointment with?"

"My old pal the flag admiral. I'm going to walk into his office, climb up on top of his desk, look down at him from on high, and demand, 'All right, Ross—what's going on?' "

"The ship ahead just transmitted a message to the asteroid's storage facility. . . . They're requesting to be resupplied with ketracel white."

"Looks like we've come to the right place."

After making her comment on Garak's observation, Dax readjusted her helm, taking greater care now that the captured Jem Hadar beetle they were hiding in was traveling in Jem Hadar space and any mismanagement of the vessel might be noticed.

Sisko appreciated the effort.

Garak continued monitoring the communication between the other Jem Hadar ship and the facility on the small asteroid they were approaching. This was it—one of the "special missions" he had wheeled out of Starfleet Command, thanks to Vice-Admiral Warner's pressure on Admiral Ross's depleted fleet condition. The ship ahead of them wanted a new supply of ketracel white to keep its crew alive, and thus moved into tighter orbit around the asteroid.

"I just saw a security net flash around the asteroid, Captain," Garak reported. "They just let that ship inside the net to be restocked."

"Keep watching, Garak," Sisko told him, battling the temptation to put a headset on and see for himself. "Don't miss any details—"

"That ship beamed down a hundred and ten empty canisters," Garak reported. "And now the storage facility is beaming up a hundred and ten full ones."

Quickly Sisko tapped his combadge. "Everything ready, Chief?"

Over the comm, Miles O'Brien answered, *"I've got eighty-three empty canisters standing by . . . and one not so empty. Ninety isotons of enriched ultritium should take out the entire storage facility and everything else within eight hundred kilometers."*

"Then we'd better be *nine* hundred kilometers away when the bomb goes—"

"The other ship is leaving orbit," Garak said.

Sisko turned. "Dax?"

"The entire exchange," she said, "took ninety-two point three seconds."

Quickly Garak tapped on his panel. "I've asked for eighty-four canisters of ketracel white. . . . Excellent! They're acknowledging my request."

Ah, the wonders of redundancy. Watching all this go on, seeing his crew exact his orders with such fluid efficiency, and having the processing station down there be so accommodating, Sisko appreciated the convenient predictability of the Jem Hadar.

He held his breath as his beetle-shaped prize moved in for its own replenishment, ticked off a few seconds, then said, "Chief, set the detonator for three minutes."

"Detonator set."

"Three minutes?" Bashir turned to him. "If it takes us ninety-two seconds to make the exchange, that doesn't leave us much time to get away."

"It doesn't give the Jem Hadar much time to detect the explosive either." By this, Sisko clearly made the doctor understand that their survival wasn't the main idea of this mission, as it may have been in other recent maneuvers. Bashir fell quiet and didn't protest as Sisko looked at Dax and said, "Beam down the canisters."

"Canisters away."

Nog looked up from his set of cylindrical monitor housings. "I hope whoever's in charge down there hasn't take a lunch break."

Nervous, Bashir uselessly said, "The Jem Hadar don't eat, Nog."

"That's good," the cadet responded. "How do we know they're Jem Hadar?"

"Relax, cadet," Dax told him. "Everything's on schedule. They've just beamed eighty-four canisters of white into our cargo hold."

Garak tapped his controls again, as he had been instructed to do. "I've acknowledged receipt and requested clearance for departure."

"Good," Sisko said. "Prepare to go to warp."

"Standing by," Dax responded.

"Captain, I think we have a problem—" Garak tensed abruptly. "They've raised their security net!"

"Repeat our request for clearance."

Tap, tap, tap—

"They're not responding."

Stepping close to Sisko, Bashir lowered his voice and quickly said, "If they don't drop the net before the bomb goes off, we don't stand a chance!"

Reliably Dax reported, "One minute thirty seconds to detonation."

As Chief O'Brien hurried onto the bridge, Nog gasped, "You think they found the bomb?"

"I doubt it," O'Brien told him, "not this fast."

The doctor looked at him. "Then why aren't they letting us go?"

"Good question." Sisko clenched his fists.

"Captain," Garak broke in, "they're responding. . . . They're ordering us to stand by."

"For what?"

"They're not saying."

"One minute fifteen seconds," Dax ticked off.

Sisko turned. "Chief, can we punch a hole through that security net?"

"Sure, but it'll take a couple minutes."

"We don't have a couple minutes. What about disabling the net's power generator?"

"The explosion'll do that," Nog grumbled.

To which Garak commented, "That won't do us much good."

From Dax—"One minute."

"Maybe it will," Sisko murmured. "When the generator is destroyed, the net'll go down. . . . All we have to do is time it so we're moving fast enough at the moment of detonation to avoid getting caught in the explosion."

Dax looked at him. "But not so fast that we smash into the net before it's deactivated."

"It's tricky," O'Brien said—not exactly a dissent.

Sisko tried to sound positive. "Not if we time it right."

Dax worked her console, feeding the idea and all the appropriate numbers into the computer. "Let's see . . . a radial geodesic in a thirty-nine Cockrane warp field contracts normal space at a rate of—"

"We have to go to full impulse one point three seconds before the bomb detonates," Julian Bashir instantly calculated. Ah, the enhanced mind.

Sisko looked up. "Dax?"

"The computer agrees with Julian."

"Of course it does," Garak quipped. "They think alike."

As Bashir grinned modestly, Dax clicked her controls. "Turning over piloting controls to the main computer. . . . Set."

"Time?"

"Twenty-two seconds until the explosion."

Nog drew a sharp breath of victory. "Twenty-two seconds. . . . That's plenty of time!"

"See, cadet?" O'Brien began. "There was nothing to worry ab—"

A booming ruckus throbbed through the ship and they were jolted hard, only staying on their feet because they were holding onto the consoles and the ship happened to tip up on its nose instead of spinning sideways. Every monitor erupted into a blown mess, recording the explosion of the facility they had just been in communication with.

The force drove the ship forward instead of incinerating it, but only because they had already been moving. Had the ship been halted in space it would've been cracked like an egg. Only their momentum in the direction of the blast saved them.

Over the roar of damage, O'Brien choked, "Must've gone off early!"

Sisko clung to a console. "Dax, get us out of here!"

On the monitors, they could all see the plume of explosion rushing toward them, then begin, with painful slowness, to pull back away from them. It was an illusion, of course—the explosion was still rushing toward them and they were barely outrunning the main surge. The shock wave—that was something else.

It caught up with them in seconds, lifting the ship from underneath and stalling the progress just enough for the explosion to catch up. Raw flame and debris engulfed the tail of the Jem Hadar vessel and chewed relentlessly. Frustration gripped Sisko—he had to control himself and leave the driving to Dax.

For a ghastly moment he doubted her ability to get them out of this. Skill couldn't always beat physics—sometimes luck was all he could—

"We're pulling away!" O'Brien encouraged.

The ship righted itself suddenly, regained its crab-like balance, and got an abrupt surge of power from somewhere.

"Not quite according to plan," Garak tensely said, "but I think Starfleet will find the results satisfactory. . . ."

"I agree, Mr. Garak." Sisko offered Dax a nod. "Well done, old man." Moving to O'Brien, he asked, "How bad is it?"

O'Brien's hands moved across his diagnostics. "Doesn't look good. . . . I'm going to have to switch to auxiliary life support . . . deflectors are down . . . guidance system is shot and . . ."

Reading the engineer's face with the advantage of familiarity, Sisko prodded, "What is it?"

"The core matrix is fried. . . . We don't have warp drive."

A cold knot landed in the middle of Sisko's stomach. Feeling suddenly exhausted, he let his shoulders sag and turned toward Dax, but her expression was hardly helpful.

Garak, predictably and rather uselessly, postured, "Forgive my ignorance, but without warp drive, how long is it going to take us to reach the nearest starbase?"

Good—all they needed was somebody to state the painfully obvious right out loud.

"A long time, Mr. Garak," Sisko told him, and confirmed what everyone was thinking.

"How long?"

What did they really need an on-board Cardassian for, anyway?

Saving Sisko the trouble, Julian Bashir offered a sour, unhopeful, utterly grim statement.

"Seventeen years, two months and . . . three days. . . . Give or take an hour."

The first requisite of a good citizen in this Republic of ours is that he shall be willing and able to pull his own weight.

Theodore Roosevelt

CHAPTER
10

CAPTAIN CHARLES REYNOLDS stood over Admiral Ross with his hands on his hips and a fully armed unflinching glare. He'd asked his questions. Now he was waiting.

"What're you talking about, Charlie?" the admiral asked. "What's going on where?"

"Border. Who've you got out there?" Reynolds swiped a hand at the star chart on the corner monitor. "Who's working the Cardassians area where I thought I was alone?"

"Charlie, I can't . . . I can't divulge other crews' assignments and you know it."

"Ever since they made you an admiral you've been the stuffedest shirt in this sector, Hal. A Jem Hadar ship came by us and didn't even shoot, didn't pursue, didn't seem interested in engaging us at all. They evaded like crazy and only fired back when we fired on them. Even then they took potshots at our weapons array like my son shooting his slingshot at birds. My son hates to hunt, Hal. He cried all night when he winged a gull. They didn't fire on our engines, not our power source—that's not how the Jem Hadar work. Who was in that ship?"

"You didn't . . . you didn't, uh . . ."

Ah-hah! Clue!

"No, we didn't kill them. We got chased out by three other Jem Hadar ships. And funny thing—real funny—good old number one never came after us at all. Never even tried. Didn't fire as we were retreating. Nothing."

"How'd you get away?"

"Brilliance and genius and all those best-of-the-best things you hear tell about. Hal, I'm in Intelligence, remember? They don't put people there who don't have some. Fess up." Reynolds heightened his force, but lowered the level of assault by sitting down in the lounge chair before the desk. "I haven't melted lately or rearranged myself into a—here."

Abruptly he picked up a small metal paperweight of a seagull on the desk and put the sharp pointed end of the wing against the palm of his hand. A little pressure, a downward swipe—

Ross jolted. "Charlie, don't do that! Stop it!"

Blood drained down Reynolds' wrist and soaked into his uniform sleeve. As it pooled and began to drip onto the gray carpet, he looked at Ross and waited.

The admiral's expression had crumpled under the

duress of the moment, and the pressures of the entire war. "All right, all right, Charlie. . . ." he sighed. "I know you're not a shapeshifter. . . ."

Widening his eyes, raising one brow and lowering the other, Reynolds gave him a look like a Halloween gargoyle, the kind he used on his crew when he wanted them to quit treating him like a captain and start treating him like somebody they actually respected.

"You guys at Command have a big bad secret," he said as blood dripped from his hand to the carpet. "Gonna let me in on it or do I have to . . . ?"

Ross seemed to feel cornered, or just worn down. Reynolds ticked off a few seconds without saying anything, letting the silence work.

"Is your hand all right?" the admiral wondered, nervously blinking at the carpet.

Pushing a finger against the cut to get it to stop bleeding, Reynolds sat back and heaved an impatient breath.

The computer bleeped with some kind of incoming information, but neither of them even glanced at it. Other than the subtle gurgle of a small aquarium on the far side of the office, there was no sound.

"It's Barnburner Sisko, right?" Reynolds prodded sharply.

Ross visibly flinched. "Charlie, why in hell would you say that?"

"Don't you mean, 'what'? Brains, that's what! Okay, here's what I know—stop me when I'm wrong. I'm charging right at 'em. They target my weapons. They got me boxed. Three behind, one in front, and somehow I get past it. The front guy doesn't pursue me. Why not? That's not how Jem Hadar work at all, not even a little bit. They don't target weapons when they can hit engines. So I add up two and two, come back to the starbase, do a personnel search, and Ben Sisko's assigned to the starbase, but he's not here. Why ain't he here, Hal?"

"Charlie . . . you're a . . . pest."

"Well, yeah!" Reynolds leaned back in the chair and shifted a couple of times. "Sisko's on a mission on my border, using a Jem Hadar ship so he can get inside and do something nasty. You guys aren't telling anybody because you're afraid your own shoes might be infiltrators."

Before him, the admiral started to sweat. A clean sheen of perspiration appeared across the lauded brow.

Reynolds took that as a victory. "I could've shot the ship out from under him and his whole crew and never even known it. Cuss it, Hal, I don't want to be the one who takes out a Starfleet crew with friendly fire. Nor does anybody else want to live with that. We're acting like a paranoid bunch of old widows instead of a coordinated military force and we're bound to pay for it the hard way. You guys at the top have got to get with the guys at Intelligence and figure out some way to know who's a shapeshifter and who's not. Or *what*'s not, or pretty soon you're going to find yourself an admiral with nobody left to be an admiral for!"

Sitting abruptly forward to the edge of his chair, Reynolds slapped his cut hand on Ross's desk smartly enough to splatter blood across the shiny surface and the padd lying there.

"You've got to clear the way for covert missions. Make some kind of code or something. Or isolate us so you know we haven't been infiltrated. Something! If Ben Sisko and that patched-together crew of his are on a search-and-destroy, you'd better tell me and let me clear the path so they can come back from it. Next time there might not be three Jem Hadar ships to come in and chase me away and I'm gonna take out anything and anybody that crosses my line of fire. So make up your mind."

Ross groaned audibly, sighed hard, then shook his head. After a moment a smile crept across his lips and he leered over the desk. "You realize I have to kill you now. . . ."

"Sure you do."

"What do you want, Charlie?"

"In."

"In?"

"I want in. Something's going on, and it's good that something's going on. It's about *time* something's going on! We can't keep backing up or we're gonna lose everything. Just like every other captain, I know we'd better do something sneaky and do it soon, because standing toe to toe with a guy bigger than you is a lousy way to fight and so far we been getting the stuffing stomped out of us, and even admirals can add."

"Long sentence. . . ."

"Yup, well, I specialize in long things, Admiral.

Long assignments, long marriage, long promises, long obligations, but I sure as blazes know I don't want to be involved in a long war. One ship with the right information and a clever plan can turn the course of a war in a way sometimes a whole fleet can't. So me and my crew want in right now while the fire's hot."

"My crew and I," Ross droned.

"Yeah, them too. It's becoming real personal for us. The Jem Hadar are almost to Blue Rocket. All our families are facing evacuation. Everything we built, all we got, it's going sour. I managed to make something that cussed few captains have for their children—an address, a real address. I want to keep it. I got eight kids, Hal. I don't want casualties and you don't want sixteen million prisoners of war to have to negotiate for. You need people like us. Me and my crew been out there on the other side. We're hardened. Everybody gutless already transferred out or died or something. We're just like Sisko and that bag of hardshelled nuts he runs around with. We unflinchingly risk our lives because we all know we're losing, and if there's some way to gain a foothold we'll all do it. We know how compartmentalized everything is because you're afraid of shapeshifters. So why risk telling somebody else? I already know. Can you tell me you have all that many people you can trust? Me and my crew, we're not kamikazes, we're not looking to die, but we're willing to. If we don't die, when it's all over I just want one thing—I want me and my crew to stay together and all of us stay assigned to Blue Rocket. You've all forgotten about us this long, so just keep forgetting. What's it gonna be, Hal? Speak, boy, speak."

The office bolted to sudden silence as Charlie stopped talking and let his words ring and ring, and well they did. Instantly the soft trill of the working computer and the ever softer gush of the air conditioning system seemed to virtually roar.

Admiral Ross glared across his desk as Charlie sat in the chair and waited. Charlie could talk, but he could wait too.

That was all of life, wasn't it? Talk, wait. Talk some more. Wait longer.

The admiral's face darkened. His tired eyes were pouched deeply now, more deeply than a few minutes ago, and his cheeks had lost their ruddy color, strangely matching the wall to a shade. One more time he sighed. This time the sigh was punctuated by a little twitch of his left eye.

"Charlie Reynolds, damn your skinny hide. . . . I wish you were a *bad* captain."

"You wanted to see me?"

As the door to his office opened and Kira Nerys drummed in on stiff legs with her hands clasped behind her narrow body, Dukat quickly put Benjamin Sisko's little white ball back on the desk and hoped she didn't see him fiddling with it.

"I always want to see you, Major," he told her, trying to sound welcoming. "And therein lies the problem. . . . It's been three months since my return to this station and we've barely spent any time with one another. Oh, I suppose you can point to the various meetings we've attended together . . . but they never seem to offer us the opporunity to venture beyond station business—"

"I don't have time for this." Kira spun in place and aimed for the door.

"Major!" Dukat spat.

She stopped, slowly turned.

Deliberately softening, Dukat attempted, "I haven't dismissed you yet."

Her eyes were like small dark stars, glossy and bright in the nebula of her pale cheeks and cropped auburn hair. "What do you want from me, Dukat?"

Such a small question, so many answers. Dukat stood and went to stand before her, sensing that having her stand while he was sitting too clearly delineated the legal relationship—not at all the angle of their association he wanted to fertilize.

"Come now, Major," he began again, "have the last three months been that bad?"

"Is that why I'm here?" Her voice was incendiary—sparking, but not quite burning yet. "To flatter you? Let you know what a good job you're doing and how happy we all are to have you back?"

Oh—now it was burning.

He moved closer. "Sarcasm doesn't become you, Major. It's your directness that I've always found appealing."

A little smolder erupted from her throat. "Dukat, I've got better things to do than stand here and help you play out one of your little fantasies."

Again she tried to move, but this time he was able

to block her way. One hand against the wall, and she was boxed in. Measuring his words, Dukat lowered his voice. "You feel I've betrayed you."

"Not just me," she bolted back. "You betrayed everyone. Including your own people."

Was that what she really thought? Did others think that? His skin grew colder.

"Cardassia was on the edge of an abyss, Major," he attempted. "The war with the Klingons turned us into a third-rate power. My people had lost their way. I've made them strong again."

"At what price? You've sold Cardassia to the Dominion!"

"A high price, to be sure," he agreed readily. "But look what we're getting in return. The Alpha Quadrant itself."

"We'll see about that," she grumbled.

"Yes, we will," he said, then changed again and offered the most ingratiating smile he could manage. He hadn't meant to strike the chord of future matters, but what else would work? "I could make things very pleasant for you here, Kira. . . ."

Her hot eyes iced over at the change of intimation. "You could start by doing something about your breath."

Forcing a laugh, Dukat actually stepped back. "I'm a patient man. I can wait."

Kira was simply boiling now, and Dukat wondered if that weren't part of her attraction—the fact that she could be made angry so easily, those passions running so near the surface. He hadn't made her mad on purpose, yet he hadn't avoided it either. She was indeed wonderful to watch, even through the veil of her hatred for him. When would that hatred melt?

"Wait for what?" she spat. "What do you think is going to happen, Dukat? You think you're going to wear me down with your charming personality? That I'm going to be swept off my feet by that insincere smile? Are you really so deluded that you actually believe we're going to have some kind of intimate relationship?"

Her skin flushed at the cheeks. He raised his hand to brush the warm skin. "We already do."

She slapped his hand away with the scythe of her arm.

Able only to close the moment with a clumsy laugh that masked his nervousness, Dukat suddenly begged escape.

"Good day, Major," he said, covering his failure at the tender arts. "I'm afraid I have work to do."

While Sisko and Dax stood by, waiting, Garak and Bashir left the bridge to do an on-sight inspection of the lower decks, and O'Brien and Nog worked at one of the main control panels. Several other crewmembers assisted on the painstaking business of diagnosing what was wrong and what to do about it, in that order. Garak kept his headset on, scanning space for intrusion, and certainly there eventually would be someone coming here to investigate loss of contact with that ketracel white facility.

And they had no way to run away from the area.

"Come on, Chief," Sisko urged, "tell me something."

On the floor, O'Brien said, "There's not much damage to the main core, but the support systems that sustain it took some bad hits. It might take a few days—"

"How many?"

"About . . . three or four, I think . . . if I don't need to fabricate too many—"

"Captain!" Garak came to life with a jolt. "One—no, two Jem Hadar fighters heading our way!"

Sisko swung to a monitor. "Chief!"

O'Brien shouted something at Dax, then Nog chimed in with his part, but Sisko was no longer paying attention to specifics. "Where are those ships now, Garak?"

"Bearing three-one-zero mark two-five-one and still closing!"

As Sisko grabbed for a headset and tried to focus the dizzying view that pierced his mind, his crew shouted back and forth about damned thruster arrays and gyrodynes and lateral matrices and damned something else. In Sisko's head the starscape whirled and spiraled, then finally got a grip on two incoming Jem Hadar ships.

"—auxiliary core—starboard console—"

"—already tried that!"

"No power—"

"Dax!" Sisko interrupted. "There's a dark-matter nebula sixty degrees above the bow! Can we reach it?"

"Yes, but that nebula's never been charted. We don't know what's in there."

Garak sputtered something about weapon's range just as the Jem Hadar ships opened fire, rocking their captured vessel with impunity. The jig was up. They'd been found out.

"Take us into that nebula, old man, full impulse!"

Another hit rocked them just as Dax wheeled the ship full about on a warp strut and gunned the engines toward the dark-matter nebula. With systems damaged, Sisko could feel the sudden acceleration dragging on his body like a thousand sticky fingers.

Just when he thought they might get a new surge of luck, a direct barrage blew every console on the bridge. A wall of light surrounded Dax and her arms flayed out like an angel's wings. Then reality came rushing back and she was on the deck ten feet back from her helm. She didn't get up.

Sisko stumbled across debris and burned carpet and came down on a knee beside her. Moisture instantly soaked into his trousers—blood. Her midsection was laid open just below the ribs. First aid wouldn't do. Her eyelids fluttered and she fought for consciousness, but she was losing. Her only organized motion was to grasp for Sisko's hand.

"Sisko to Bashir—medical emergency!"

The headset still pumped information into his mind, a ghastly picture of the dark-matter nebula surging toward them as the pilotless ship careened in wild flight on its latest course. The course was laid in, but there was no control. That meant the nearest source of gravity could easily yank them into it. A merciless barrage from the attacking ships knocked Sisko sideways and the headset fell off and tumbled into the rubbish that moments ago had been the helm.

Reality jammed into a blur. . . . Dax tried to speak,

Sisko uttered useless encouragements which instantly dissolved into forgetfulness, Bashir arrived and gave her something for the pain but obviously could do little here to mend the gash. The ship was kicked relentlessly again and again, then quite abruptly the attack stopped and another hard hit came, but this one was from forward.

How could that be? Had they hit a wall in space?

"Sensors are gone!" O'Brien called. "Impulse engines off line—in fact, everything's off line. . . . Emergency power is holding for now—"

"Garak," Sisko called, "take a look outside!"

The Cardassian struggled to get his own headset up and working, muttering, "Just a moment. . . ."

Sisko twisted to O'Brien. "What happened?"

The engineer's pale face screwed into a mask. "Not sure—we might've been hit by some kind of gravitational spike in the—"

But Garak cut him off.

"Hang on!"

CHAPTER

11

"YOU SHOULD'VE SEEN the arrogant, smug look on his face. He was in control and there was nothing I could do about it! The war isn't over yet, but as far as Dukat's concerned, he's already won. I'd love to show him he's wrong."

Kira Nerys stalked the floor of Odo's office, still broiling and twitching, and wishing she could be honest about Dukat's underlying motives regarding her personally—but how could she tell Odo something like that? Knowing how he also felt about her? What was all this? Was she wearing the wrong perfume?

I don't wear perfume . . .

"I'm afraid," Odo responded with his gravelly voice, "for the time being at least, he *has* won. Look at me. I don't know why I bother to sit here every day.

I don't even have a security force to patrol the Promenade."

Stopping in her tracks, Kira looked at him. "Then ask for one! Demand that they reinstate your Bajoran deputies."

"Dukat will never agree to that."

"Forget Dukat," she told him. If only that were possible. "Go directly to Weyoun. He'll listen to you. In his eyes, you're a god. That gives you power!"

Odo was watching her intently. The fact that he didn't respond right away proved that she might be on the right track. Yes, of course! He had a natural advantage! Why weren't they using it?

"What good is having power unless you're willing to use it?" she pressed. "He worships Founders, you're one of them—"

His unsculpted chin rose an inch. "I am certainly not one of them."

"No, no, I didn't mean that," she backpedaled. "But you know what I do mean."

"Yes. . . . I suppose there's no avoiding reality. I am what I am . . . physically, anyway. . . ."

"And to Weyoun, you are what you look like. Go in there, Odo. *Be* a Founder. Get your authority back. We need it. Get up. I'll walk you there."

The whole process of requesting an audience with the great Weyoun, Vorta and representative of the Dominion, made Odo wish to melt into a puddle and slip into a crack somewhere. Even more disgusting, Odo caught the end of a conversation between Weyoun and Dukat as he was led in by Damar.

". . . the Founders are the masters. I am merely their servant. As are the Jem Hadar. And you."

"That may be, but even amongst the servants, someone has to be in charge."

"That's exactly the kind of observation I've come to expect from you, Dukat. Interesting, yet somewhat petty."

Odo almost turned around and left, but Damar was already announcing their presence. "Forgive the interruption. But he insisted on seeing you immediately."

Odo glanced at Damar. He had made no demands about immediacy. Perhaps the urgency was Damar's. Did the assistant Cardassian not enjoy seeing his Gul shunted to inferiority by the Vorta?

Making a note to remember that, Odo stopped moving forward as Weyoun floated toward him, arms outstretched, as if he meant to commit the gravity of an embrace.

"Founder," the Vorta mewled. "I'm honored by your visit. Is there some way I can be of service?"

"I want my Bajoran security officers reinstated," Odo flatly said.

Weyoun bowed his head in reverence. "Consider it done."

Oh . . . much too easy.

But might as well enjoy. "From now on they'll be responsible for security on the Promenade."

"I don't see any problem with that."

Unable to use all the arguments he had been storing up, Odo found himself simply staring at the subservient Vorta's milky violet eyes, and found himself being nauseatingly appreciated in return.

"I do."

Ah—a hint of reality. Odo turned to Dukat.

And so did Weyoun, with a hard look and a silencing hand. "This is between me and Odo, Dukat. I'll thank you to keep out of it."

Then he smiled.

The smile was really too much to continue gazing upon. Odo turned to Damar. "I'll have my officers report to the armory within the hour."

Damar stiffened, obviously blistered at the idea of actually arming Bajorans on the station that Cardassians had just wrested from them, and he shot a glower at Dukat, but the Gul bit his tongue and nodded. Damar was being given no quarter to refuse.

With nothing more to say, Odo turned to leave.

Now the Vorta stepped to him before he had completely turned. "Now that I've done something for you . . ."

Odo turned back.

"Perhaps," Weyoun continued, "there's something you'd consent to do for me."

Feeling his entire body temperature drop a degree or two, Odo remained silent.

The Vorta turned a shoulder to Dukat and Damar, dismissing the two Cardassians with a subtle gesture. "We would be honored to have you join us as the rulers of this station."

"Rulers?" Odo repeated.

"Yes," Weyoun said. "The station's ruling council. You, me, and Dukat."

"Absolutely not!" Dukat came to life suddenly, and swung on Weyoun. "Are you out of your—do you realize what it took to get control of this station away from Bajoran and Federation sympathies?"

"Odo is neither Barjoran nor one of those Federation races, Dukat. He is a Founder. We cannot put ourselves above him in any way, here or elsewhere."

"Ridiculous!"

"Even so."

There was no getting out of it. Odo sourly realized he'd been maneuvered, or counter-maneuvered at least. The question became whether he wanted his armed security force more than he wanted to kick Weyoun's face into the wormhole.

Still . . . even such a maneuver offered other chances.

"Will you do it?" Weyoun asked. "Will you please?"

Kira narrowed her eyes, which was difficult because somehow she was gawking at the same time.

"A member of the station's ruling council? You?"

The noise of Quark's bar provided adequate cover as she sat there with Odo, but Kira still felt as if anyone looking at her could easily have read her mind from a distance.

"Along with Weyoun and Dukat," Odo said. "Now I'll have a voice in station policy."

That sounded almost plausible, which made it harder to believe. "Are you sure this is a good idea?" she asked him.

"Dukat thought it was a terrible idea," Odo countered, as if that were a good point. "You should've seen his face when Weyoun offered me the position."

Actually, it wasn't a bad point. But it also wasn't enough.

She leaned closer across the table, only remembering at the last moment to restrain her body language. "Don't you see Weyoun's using you? Your presence on the council validates the Dominion's control of the station!"

Odo crossed his legs and tilted his shoulders in a way that told her he had just been insulted. "I thought *we* were using *him.*" He paused long enough to communicate to her that he needn't any lessons on play and counterplay—he understood the gameboard's options. "I know the dangers, Major. I've had to walk this line before, during the Cardassian occupation. I can do it again. . . . But this time I won't be alone. I'll have you to help me."

Withdrawing the scolding nature of her questions, Kira reached out and lay her hand across his. "That's right . . . you will."

His artificial mask softened. "Then this is a victory after all."

"I suppose it is," she murmured, "but for some reason, it doesn't feel like one. I wish we weren't obligated to be here. . . . It's got to be awful for you. At least I can tell myself I'm sticking up for my planet and my people."

"They're my people too," Odo quietly reminded, and Kira was suddenly embarrassed. "Bajor is another of the many unfortunate localities who happened to be near a point of contention. All through history, yours, mine, everyone's, there have been those caught with something valuable in their front yard. They didn't make it, they don't want it . . . yet they must defend it or be overrun. That is us, Major . . . and something will happen to change all this somehow. Because now we are in the Federation's front yard. Soon the knocking of Cardassia and the Dominion will waken the sleeping giants inside . . . and help will come. Help will come. . . ."

CHAPTER
12

"READY . . . *heave!* Ready . . . *heave!*"

Shoreline. Skies, rocks, sand, blue ocean lapping up against a cliffside. After years of life in space, this was like a dream inside their nightmare. In the middle of the bay, the captured Jem Hadar ship lay nosed into the water, half submerged in sandy muck.

Ben Sisko urged his surviving crewmen to haul their makeshift raft up the sandy shoal to the water's edge. All hands who were alive when the ship crashed were now accounted for. . . . Himself, O'Brien, Bashir, and Lieutenant Neeley hauling this makeshift raft cobbled together with barrels, conduit, cables, and loaded with what little salvage they could toss out—phasers, tricorders, jackets, and the blanketed form of Jadzia Dax, tied to the raft and blessedly unconscious.

"Ready . . . *heave!*"

Nog, already on the shore. Garak standing over him. Ensign Gordon on his hands and knees on the beach, coughing up seawater and fighting for consciousness.

Sisko envied them. He wanted to be on the warm sand. He wanted to lie down and relax his knotted neck, let his legs go limp, unclench his hands.

"One more! Ready—*heave!*"

Sand scratched under the raft, rattling Sisko from his spine to his shoulders. They'd made it. Grounded.

"How . . . how is she?" Sisko gasped.

Not nearly as exhausted as everyone else, Bashir scanned Dax's quiet body with his medical tricorder. "Stable for now. Garak! I need a hand!"

"Bloody hell!"

Who was that? Oh, who else? O'Brien.

"What?" Sisko demanded.

"I can't believe it!"

"What?"

"I tore my pants!"

"You tore your pants . . . ?"

The sheer tragic irony in his own voice made Sisko grin. Then the grin caught a spark and he was chuckling.

"That's right. . . ." O'Brien tugged at the lips of his trouser leg, torn halfway up the outside hem.

That was funny. It was hilarious. The two of them fell back against the damned raft and let the joke roll through them. Torn trousers. A rip in the fabric of the universe!

Shipwrecked. Beached. Down.

"You all right otherwise, Chief?" Sisko gasped

when he'd caught more of his breath. "Whatever ripped your pants didn't rip you, did it?"

"Let's see . . . shipwrecked on a quirky little planet inside a dark nebula with a little white sun and a possibility of starvation. . . . No, I'm just dandy otherwise."

With a lingering chuckle, Sisko shoved himself around and stood up on his shuddering legs. On the beach, Garak and Bashir were settling Dax into a rock's shadow. It *was* bright here . . . where there was sun and water, there would have to be food. And they'd salvaged a few days' worth of survival rations.

He glanced into the sky. "A little chilly despite the brightness. Might be downright cold when that sun goes down. We'd better find some shelter."

Squinting, and holding his pants closed with one hand, O'Brien scanned the rocky seawall north of them. "I see caverns in those cliffs. Maybe there are caves on the dry side."

"Good bet. We've got to keep Dax warm. I wish that diagnostic bed could float." He turned and looked back at the sinking Jem Hadar ship that had so recently been their hope and home. The ship rotated slowly in the water, one wing low, while the sea crept quickly up the exposed hull. "How deep did you say it was out there?"

"Three to five hundred meters, depending on the topography of the seafloor."

"Guess we won't be making any free dives."

"Let Julian do it. He can probably hold his genetically enhanced breath to fifty fathoms."

"You're all heart, Chief. Help me beach this raft."

"Aren't we beached? It's completely—"

"There might be a tide. I want to get this up on the sand and get off this open beach before anybody sees us."

O'Brien's face screwed up into a snarl. "Who in God's green meadow is going to see us?"

"We got in some good shots on those Jem Hadar. At the last minute Nog thought he saw one of them spiral in after us, on almost the same trajectory. I think they crashed. If they hit the water too, they might be alive."

"Well, with a little luck they hit a rock instead."

"We can't count on luck, Chief. Now, get a grip on the raft and let's go. *Heave!*"

CHAPTER
13

ALIEN SHORELINE. Workable planet—breathable atmosphere, enough light, too much light, a surface which could be moved upon. Moving on foot is troublesome. Jem Hadar are not constructed for infantry, but for space battle. Walking about is a tiresome business. Moving on foot must be kept to matters of practicality. The ship is irretrievable, bottomed in one of this planet's deep pools.

Third Remata'Klan. Engaging unfamiliar emotions. Concern. The future—unsure. The Vorta injured. That is critical. . . . Jem Hadar without a Vorta are directionless. Who will distribute the white if the Vorta dies? How can Jem Hadar soldiers make an injured Vorta heal?

Response: revert to procedure. Patrol. Study. Conclude. Act.

Fourth Limara'Son approaching.

"We have established a defense perimeter around the entrance to the cavern," came the report from the other soldier. "I have sent out two patrols to reconnoiter the shoreline in both directions."

Take that in, digest it, say nothing. Facts require no response. Look at the crashing surf . . . so unnatural.

Limara'Son. "The Vorta's condition has worsened. He will die soon."

Remata'Klan. "What about the First and the Second?"

Opaque sensations. Worry. Uncertainty was not familiar at all. This must be uncertainty. Was it also weakness? Inability to change occurrences?

Limara'Son. "I vaporized their bodies myself and redistributed their equipment to the rest of the men."

Good. Actions had been taken, positive movements forward. Some of the uncertainty faded.

Limara'Son. "You are now the First."

"No. I questioned the Vorta's orders. He will not forget that. As long as he lives, I will remain Third."

"You were right to question him. If he hadn't ordered us into the nebula two days ago, we would not have crashed—"

"It was not my place! Remember . . . 'Obedience brings victory.'"

Limara'Son accepting the axiom. "'And victory is life.'"

Suitably humbled. Good. The situation began to gain ballast.

Crashing seas. Wind and air . . . an uneasy eternalness without purpose . . .

Remata'Klan. "Until we re-establish communication, we will hold this world for the Dominion."

"And if we cannot re-establish communication?"

"Then we will hold this world for the Dominion until we die."

Back to the base camp. A wet, cloying environment, but cover from the natural elements outside. A hiding place, defensible, functional. Comfort was no legitimate factor.

All soldiers occupied, working on communication sytem, stripping and cleaning weapons which had been submersed in that pool. Clumsy movement . . . nervous twitching. Tools being dropped, fingers trembling. Glances of distraction.

They are all suffering from lack of white. Neck tubes were all gurgled nearly dry now.

A small fire for light, and to keep the Vorta warm. The fire struggles in the big cave, only a tiny source against the bigger moist darkness. The Vorta upon his mat, raised on rock slabs. He seems pained, if pain can be seen. Misery creasing his pale features. Dark hair grayed with dust and crusted salt from the pool of surf.

The Vorta. Looking at Remata'Klan. "This must be . . . quite gratifying for you . . . but I've decided not to give you the pleasure of . . . watching me die in this foul-smelling cavern. I intend to . . . live."

"I understand."

"How long is it until we re-establish communication?"

"Seventh Yak'Talon estimates it will take at least ten days before we can attempt a low-power test."

A crease in the Vorta's forehead. "Ten days. . . ."

He seems exhausted. Now his eyes are closed. What is he thinking? If he dies, will Remata'Klan become First? Distribute the white?

Remata'Klan. "It is time for the white."

An acquiescing gesture from the Vorta, and a wave of his hand toward the black container. A nod from Remata'Klan, and a soldier brings the precious case to the Vorta, who works the security lock, finally, wrenching the scorched and battered top upward.

Remata'Klan cannot see inside the case. Looking around would suggest distrust for the Vorta.

Other soldiers gather around, waiting for their dose of white. Soon the weakness will be gone, the twitching, the trembling, the hunger and dizziness. The fears and cramps.

The Vorta. "Third Remata'Klan . . . can you vouch for the loyalty of your men?"

Part of the white ritual. Only one answer.

"We pledge our loyalty to the Founders from now until death."

"Then receive this reward from the Founders. May it keep you strong."

The first vial goes to Remata'Klan. The second—

But the Vorta is closing the case. He's locking the case.

Limara'Son. "Only one?"

Remata'Klan. "Keep your place!"

Anxiety from the soldiers—so little white between them? One vial?

"This case of white must last until we're rescued." The Vorta. "At least ten days. Possibly more. I will ration the supply. Don't worry. I am the Vorta . . . I will take care of you all."

A nod from Remata'Klan, and turn, then gesture to all the soldiers that they should go back to their work. Work was everything. Work, patrol, survive, defend.

Behind, the Vorta lies injured. Perhaps dying. Alone.

Caverns, cold and forbidding. Moisture leaked down the shale walls. Flat-faced bits of mica glistened and made tiny rainbows on black surfaces. Sisko thought of the black lacquer desk in his office on *Deep Space Nine*, and the lamps glowing there. There was no source of warmth at all, not even from the single leg of sunshine leaning in the narrow opening. The light bent upward a meter, then quickly failed.

Sisko made the decision, with some internal struggle, to use one of the phasers to heat the standing rocks on the ground, where they were partly insulated and would hold the energy for a while. He had to be sparing—they might need the phaser as weapons later. If they were to be here any extended amount of time, they'd have to build shelter, find something to burn, find something to eat. Survival came down to those three things. Home, heat, food.

The waterlogged crew busied themselves and didn't complain, even turning to a gallows humor to bolster the soggy moment. Everyone stripped out of the wet uniforms, after Sisko's second order, and laid them on the hot rocks. He didn't want anyone getting pneumonia and taking Bashir's attention away from Dax. Soon the cavern was moist with steam from the process. The clothing dried quickly enough, as Starfleet ordnance was constructed to do, but the boots stayed wet a long time, forcing them to pick around barefoot on the gravelly sand. Nog inventoried the stuff they'd managed to salvage. Neeley and Gordon checked the integrity of their cavern for hidden exits that might have to be guarded, or structural instability that might fall in on them. Garak mended O'Brien's trousers. Bashir tended Dax as well as possible with very limited medical equipment. Sisko—his job was to worry.

He realized he was in trouble when he made a foolish promise to the drowsy Dax. He promised to get her out of here.

How? An uncharted rock inside an uncharted nebula, in Cardassian space after having come in here without logging the voyage, flying a captured enemy ship. Get out?

When would he learn to stop making promises? Promise Dad to get Jake off the station . . . he couldn't make good on that one either. Now he was stuck here, as trapped as any pre-spaceflight Neanderthal, on a protoplanet in the middle of, quite literally, nothing. And nobody knew where they were. Nobody but possibly the enemy. Great. Make more promises.

Dax. . . . Her face was so pale, threaded with pain, reduced to the universal prescription of rest and relying upon her own natural healing powers, if any. Julian Bashir had certainly done all he could do and probably a few things he conjured from sheer cleverness, but there simply wasn't much more than a rescue kit and a medical tricorder. Dax was down and she was going to stay down for a while. The only favor Sisko could do for her was pretend he didn't need her advice, that she could relax and he would muddle through.

As his clothing dried he fretted about the situations here and on DS9. How were Kira and Odo doing, back under the control of Gul Dukat, and with the added irritant of the slimy, soft-spoken Vorta? Every Jem Hadar crew of any size had a Vorta on board to manage them. The cool-blooded genetically engineered master running the hot-blooded genetically engineered vassals. A soup not meant to be stirred.

And Cardassians for spice. Would Kira and Odo dare tinker with the status quo on the station? Mixed feelings rushed through Sisko. What would he do? Sit there under the treaty and bide time? Make nice with the Cardassians and the Vorta in order to keep Bajor and the station from becoming targets?

Maybe. But Kira was a former freedom fighter and Odo had lived long and hard under the oppression of the Cardassians. Could he expect them to be passive now? Complicitors in their own minds?

No "maybe" about it—he'd take some kind of action. Some underlying subversion. He knew what he would do, and yet he also hoped Kira and Odo wouldn't do that. Odd, to have these tumbling feelings, to field a dozen plots and tricks in his mind yet not be able to act upon them or even know if acting upon them would be the right thing to do. He'd left Bajor and DS9 in a certain condition because he wanted them to survive. He expected his friends to understand what he wanted and hold back their quite justified reactions. Was he asking too much of them? With communication cut off completely, how could he know what was happening?

And Jake was there, barely out of his teens, inexperienced, feisty, trying to prove himself in the trenches. . . . What would happen to the son of the emissary of Bajor if Kira, a Bajoran, and Odo, a shapeshifter thought to be a deity by the Vorta, took action against the Dominion? Sisko knew he had created a problem for Kira and Odo just by arranging a treaty between Bajor and the Dominion. Yes, the move saved Bajor from attack, but it also put Bajor and the station at the mercy of the Dominion. There would be no more trade with outside sources, no inflow of repair parts, medical supplies, food, technical help. The planet and the station would be forced to turn to the Dominion for support, and that would strengthen the Dominion's position. The leaders of the planetary population would deeply resent that. The Vedeks particularly would bristle at any hint of Dominion occupation over what they saw as their spiritual territory.

Gul Dukat would know all that and be ready to respond with a hard slap to any protests. Not a good situation, and it would never become good. Bajor or the station would break, or Kira would break or Odo would melt. Something would go wrong. The balance would be broken and everything would spin out of control.

Somehow, eventually, that station had to be recaptured.

Thoughts of loss and insurgence bucked and sizzled in Sisko's mind. Frustration boiled in him as he had never known it before. He was stuck here, unable to do anything or know what anyone else was doing. For so many years he had juggled many baseballs, and now he only had this one little stitch to mend. His universe had contracted from a whole sector, a big populated planet, a crowded station, and the doorway between two quadrants to this handful of survivors, this tiny rock they were on, a desolate strip of surf and sand, a sunken Jem Hadar wreck, and a few days' worth of rations. And both challenges were dauntingly equal—that was the strange part.

"Mr. Gordon," he said, breaking his miserable thoughts, "Take Lieutenant Neeley and scout the terrain north of here. Mr. Garak, Cadet Nog, you two go south-east along the ridge. Look for fresh water, edible vegetation, edible animals, possibly dangerous animals, toxins . . . what else?"

"Jem Hadar," O'Brien piped.

"Oh . . . yes, do keep an eye out for Jem Hadar."

"Why should we?" Nog impulsed.

"Because I told you to, Cadet."

The boy blinked as if he'd been slapped. "Oh . . . yes, sir."

Sending Nog with Garak might be a mistake. They had an uneasy history. All right, they had a downright hostile history. Come to think of it, that was as good a reason to send them together as it was *not* to send them together.

Off they went, leaving Sisko, O'Brien, Bashir and

the drowsy Dax in the dampness together. Light from outside was changing—how long was the day on this tiny excuse for a planet? The air was a little thinner than Sisko was used to, but air was air. Between sea and space, anything breathable would do.

After two hours, Sisko was ready to start giving himself a manicure if he didn't get a report pretty damned soon from his field operatives. He had been watching O'Brien fiddle with a piece of Dominion equipment, just one of a dozen bits of circuitry they'd tossed onto the raft at the last moment. To keep himself from running out there and doing the crew's jobs for them, Sisko fixated on O'Brien's work.

"What's that?" he asked.

"With a little luck," the engineer said by way of an answer, "I might be able to hardwire one of our combadges into this sensor relay. That would give us a crude transmitter, but no power source."

Without bothering to point out that they had nobody friendly in this sector to transmit to, Sisko asked, "What about draining one of our phasers?"

"I thought about that. But I'd need a converter to bridge the two power cells, and I can't build a converter without an ion exchange matrix."

Sisko didn't respond. It didn't matter—right now they needed all the phasers, at least until they cased the area and made sure there were no hostile forces lurking here. Contacting rescue parties was a far-flung and slim chance, therefore not their first priority. Their first priority was to stay alive right now, down here, for as long as possible.

Ensign Gordon saved him from having to voice any

of that by striding in with sand on his uniform and a worried look on his face.

"Captain, I think we may have a problem. Garak and Nog haven't reported in yet and they're not answering my hails."

"How long since they reported in?"

"We contacted each other at fourteen hundred, sir. It's been over an hour, and we agreed to contact hourly."

"Where's Neeley?"

"She's on guard outside, sir. We haven't seen anything. . . . Living, I mean."

"All right, form up. Doctor, we're going out on a search party. Let's hope it doesn't turn out to be a rescue party."

The shoreline was wide and open—too wide, too bright, too easy to be seen. It was also the way Garak and Nog had gone and the only passable ground in this direction.

The search party was widely spread out across the beach to avoid providing a tempting cluster for a single shot. All personnel had their phasers drawn, except Neeley, who was handling a tricorder, tracking the infrared remnants of Garak and Nog's footprints. Unfortunately, for long stretches of beach, the footprints had been washed away by cooling licks of tide.

"Captain." Neeley slowed her pace to let Sisko catch up to her, keeping her eyes on her tricorder. "There's a group of life-forms up on the cliff . . . range seventy-five meters . . . elevation thirty meters."

Casually Sisko glanced around the whole beach,

deliberately not focusing on the location Neeley had specified. Keeping his voice too low to be picked up by sensors, he muttered, "That's where I'd be. . . . Are they Jem Hadar?"

"I think so."

"Well, let's not make it easy for them. Tell the chief to head for that large outcropping of rocks at ten o'clock. But we need to walk . . . not run."

Without any overt moves, Neeley picked up her pace and caught up with O'Brien. After a moment, O'Brien paused, pretended to get his bearings, then led the party toward the surge of rocks encrusting part of the beach, just under the ridge. No one looked up, nor indicated in any way that they knew they were being watched. Sisko kept his eyes focused ahead. Neeley continued pretending to scan. O'Brien moved slowly toward the protection of the bigger rocks, but Sisko noticed the engineer's finger was already on his phaser trigger.

Just a few more seconds . . . just a few more steps to protection, to a defensible position—

Part of the rock in front of O'Brien opened with a sharp explosion. Energy blast!

"Move!" Sisko shouted. "Go! Go! Go!"

He grabbed Neeley, who was still trying to pretend they hadn't been seen, hadn't been fired upon, and with her he dashed to the rock face, firing as he ran. Above them, he caught a glimpse of a stony Jem Hadar face, and then another blast.

"We're pinned down," he choked. "Fire at will!"

He thought of tossing in a sentence about firing

accurately and not wasting shots because the phasers were all they had, but this wasn't the time. The rock face was being chewed away by free fire from the Jem Hadar and his people had their hands full just keeping their heads from being shot off. They were in the defensive position, lower than the Jem Hadar and able only to lay down restraining fire. The Jem Hadar soldiers, pumped up and brain-clouded with the taste of victory in their single-minded way, were firing their disruptors murderously, cutting into the fissures and shearing away huge portions of the cliff that were protecting Sisko and his crew. If that was their plan, not to just hit the crew but also knock away the protective rocks, it was working.

Sheets of rock slid away, making a percussive rattle, then crashing to the sands below.

A Jem Hadar voice roared from above. "Terminate fire!"

But the disruptor fire didn't terminate—it kept up at the same vicious pace.

"Terminate!"

Some of the shooting did stop, Sisko noticed then, but somebody up there was still trigger-happy.

"You've been ordered to stop!"

Probably the "First" Jem Hadar, or whoever was leading that team. Apparently he was having trouble getting control over his men. Good, that might help. And it might be a clue—if they were castaway here, were they running out of ketracel white? Losing mental control? Going through withdrawal?

O'Brien and . . . who was that—Gordon—were

still firing on the Jem Hadar position. Sisko didn't yet order them to stop. If the Jem Hadar were indeed in the first stages of withdrawal, the harassment, or even the stubbornness, of the Starfleet team could irritate them into dissention.

Yes—they were arguing. He heard them, but the specific words were guttural, muffled.

"—reduced to Sixth!"

"—shroud . . . base camp."

"—suppression fire . . . —draw."

Draw? Withdraw, maybe? Were they pulling back? Why?

They had a superior position. Why would they pull back?

The answer might be as simple as some set of orders they had received and weren't supposed to mangle. They weren't engineered to be too independently thinking. Obedience was everything, spontaneity was not encouraged, and such minds could be confused.

He let O'Brien and the others keep firing until he was sure the Jem Hadar were no longer returning the shots.

"They're pulling out," O'Brien called.

Sisko almost told him to keep quiet, but changed his mind. "Looks that way to me."

"Why aren't they camouflaged?"

"Good question. Let's hope the answer is something in our favor. Cease fire! Lieutenant Neeley?"

"Sir!"

"Are they there, or are they gone?"

"Not reading them in the immediate vicinity anymore, sir, although some of my readings are garbled. I think this tricorder got bumped or something."

"They're not up there anymore?"

"No, sir, no life-form readings within—"

"Take a position where you can read the top of the ridge."

"Yes, sir."

"All hands, disperse and meet back at the cavern."

Two hostages. A good event.

Remata'Klan. "Kneel before the Vorta."

How strange it seemed that the Vorta had no satisfaction in his face at seeing these two captives from the Federation ship they had been chasing. Now it was confirmed, for these two were here, that that ship had crashed also. The Vorta's condition—was it worse? How could a Jem Hadar judge a being like a Vorta?

The two Federation captives on their knees. No speaking yet.

The Vorta. "How many . . . others . . . are there in your unit?"

"Nog!" The Ferengi. "Cadet third class! Serial number CX dash nine-three-seven-three dash—"

"Shut up!" The other captive. The Cardassian one. "As I tried to explain to your men, my name is Kamar and I'm a member of the Cardassian Intelligence Bureau, what used to be known as the Obsidian order. A week ago, while performing my duties in the glorious service of the Founders, I was captured by the U.S.S. Centaur. I was being held aboard one of their shuttles when we were forced to hide in his dark matter nebula by the unexpected appearance of a Dominion battleship. The shuttle was then hit by—"

"Excuse me, Mr. Kamar." The Vorta. "If that's really your name. . . . But if you're one of our allies, why were you wearing this?"

A Starfleet combadge. A change in the Cardassian's behavior. A stare at the combadge. . . .

"I was hoping you weren't going to ask me about that."

"I have only one further question for you. Is there a doctor in your unit?"

The Cardassian. "Yes."

"Garak!" The Ferengi.

Now the Cardassian's real name was known. The rest, assumably, also lies.

"Don't be too hard on him, young man." The Vorta. "He just saved your life. Take them to a secure area. Third . . ." Soldiers taking away the two captives. "I have a mission for you. All our lives may depend on it. Can I trust you to carry out my orders without question?"

Remata'Klan. A purpose. A mission. No more void moments. "My life is pledged to the service of the Dominion."

"Good. I want you to find the Starfleet unit. But do *not* engage them. Locate them, assess their strength, then report back to me."

"I understand."

"No, you don't. But that's all right. It's not important that you understand. Only that you carry out my instructions precisely."

"'Obedience brings victory.'"

"Yes. Yes, it does. . . . Go."

A good approach. Without detection even in the brightness of this nebular sun glaring down upon this planet. Starfleet officers on the low ground, Remata'Klan and soldiers up here, on the rocks, a tactical advantage. . . .

A burst of weapons fire! Against orders! The Vorta had ordered not to engage! Who is firing?

Two . . . three Jem Hadar, firing on the Starfleeters!

Return fire vomiting back up the rocks. The Starfleeters are fighting back. The Vorta's orders must stand until he dies!

Neck tube sucking again . . . the dizziness getting worse. Cramps and shaking in the fingers and knees. . . .

"Terminate fire!" Remata'Klan. "Terminate fire!"

The men drunk with murderous fury, still firing downward, confused, drilling the rocks without even hitting a targeted enemy. Waste of weapon energy!

Remata'Klan—strike down the nearest Jem Hadar. Nearby, Limara'Son now looks up, stops firing, seems to waken from the rushing confusion. Beyond him, another Jem Hadar hears nothing, ignores orders, keeps firing down again and again. Only the roar of the weapons and the sucking horror of their empty neck tubes—deafening.

Limara'Son, turning his own weapon on that other soldier. "You've been ordered to stop!"

A great effort, and the soldier stops firing.

Starfleet still firing upward, looking for cover, blasting the cliffs to rock fragments. The soldiers are unhappy about restraint. This curtails forward movement of actions, a chance at getting more white. The universe was closing in. At first, there had been war. Purpose. Orders. Then only a ship. Then only a planet. Now only the white. The tunnel closed and closed. Soon there would be only the insanity of withdrawal, and the Vorta would die and they would go insane trying to get the box open.

Remata'Klan. "Your orders were clear! You were not to engage the enemy! Who fired first?"

All silent.

Limara'Son, finally. "I did."

Disappointment. Remata'Klan. "You are reduced to Sixth. We will shroud and return to base camp—"

Explosion on the rocks. Blistering pain. . . . Remata'Klan's arm bleeding.

Limara'Son. "I can no longer shroud myself."

All the others too. No more shroud energy left anywhere. No more protection.

Remata'Klan. "You and you will provide suppression fire as we withdraw."

Limara'Son. "Understood."

Pull back carefully, while Limara'Son and the Ninth open fire again on the Starfleet position. A pause. . . . Crouch for a moment of watching the movements below.

Limara'Son. "Remata'Klan . . . I regret my disobedience."

Regrets. There were so many. Surely they stood beneath this sun and glare because of errors. Remata'Klan's hand on Limara'Son's shoulder for balance. Stand and move out to follow the others back to base camp.

Remata'Klan. "Follow us in ninety seconds. We will face the Vorta's fury together."

"Why were my orders disobeyed?"

The cave has an echo. Even injured and dying, the Vorta has a piercing voice.

Remata'Klan. "Lack of white produces anxiety among us. One man could not restrain himself when he saw the enemy."

"Which man?"

"I have dealt with the matter."

"I asked for his name."

"He is my responsibility."

"His name!"

At the side, Limara'Son waits to be betrayed. But if obedience is victory, is not loyalty success?

"I may not be First." Remata'Klan. "But I am the unit leader. You can discipline me, but only I discipline the men. That is the order of things."

The Vorta is angry, but also fatigued. He cannot struggle or resist. Things had to be in order.

The Vorta. "Very well. I leave him to you."

Success? A tactical win for Remata'Klan? Would the Vorta give them more white now?

A glance at the unit. "Dismissed."

It's well that they leave quickly, before the Vorta's pain makes him change his mind.

"You've done well, Third." The Vorta. "You may yet become First. Now . . . I have a new task for you."

* * *

"All right, it's pretty clear now that we've got a problem. Until we know if they have any weaknesses, we have to assume they don't. Come down here, Chief."

Drawing in the sandy flats of the cave floor, Sisko crouched with O'Brien and made a sketch of the surrounding area.

"We'll set up three defensive positions," he said, glancing at O'Brien. "You and Ensign Gordon on the south ridge, Lieutenant Neeley near the lava tube, Bashir and I in the dunes."

From the slab behind him, Dax murmured, "I'll stay here and guard my clothes."

He smiled, and was immediately interrupted by a comm call.

"Neeley to Captain Sisko."

"Go ahead."

"A Jem Hadar soldier has just approached my position, sir. He says he wants to talk to you alone."

"Understood. Stand by. And don't turn your back on that soldier."

"Standing by."

He eyed O'Brien. "What do you suppose that means?"

"A Jem Hadar with a superior position and a tactical advantage wanting to parlay?" O'Brien tipped his head thoughtfully. "I'd say they want to make a deal, they must need something pretty badly. We ought to let 'em suffer."

"I'd like to, but you're forgetting something."

"What am I forgetting?"

"Nog and Garak. They haven't reported in. That Jem Hadar might be here to negotiate a hostage deal."

"If they've got Nog and Garak, you'll have to be careful."

"Cunning is what I have to be. More than they are."

"Not very hard, sir."

"No, but if they've got a Vorta with them, that changes everything."

"Are you really going to meet him by yourself, sir?"

"I'd better. But . . . there's one thing I can do to seem to have an upper hand. Sisko to Neeley."

"Neeley."

"Tell the Jem Hadar representative that I will meet with him, but in our cavern, which will be his prison if his words fail to advance our situation to mutual advantage."

He knew the Jem Hadar was standing right there, listening. Neeley acknowledged, and Sisko turned to O'Brien. "Take Bashir and Gordon and stand guard in a half-circle perimeter, but stay out of sight."

"Out of sight, aye, sir."

It took Neeley ten minutes to bring the Jem Hadar representative into the cavern, even though it was only a two minute walk—and that was good thinking. Sisko hadn't been able to say anything to her over the comm, but hoped she knew procedure. Never lead an enemy directly to your camp. Make the route as complicated and unrememberable as possible.

Here they were. . . .

On the slab over there, Dax remained still and pretended to sleep, but she wasn't sleeping. Sisko silently motioned for Lieutenant Neeley to make herself scarce. Then he faced the jagged features of the Jem Hadar.

"I'm Captain Benjamin Sisko," he said simply.

"Third Remata'Klan. Two members of your unit are being held at our base camp. We will exchange them for you and your doctor."

Suddenly several pieces of the puzzle clicked into place. Sisko controlled his expression, pretending he realized nothing.

"Why do you need a doctor?"

"The Vorta has been severely wounded."

"And why me?"

"The Vorta wishes to speak to you."

"It sounds like he wants to trade two low-ranking prisoners for two more valuable ones. Would you accept a deal like that?"

"No."

"Then why should I?"

"You shouldn't."

"You're not a very good negotiator, are you?"

"I was not sent to negotiate," the Jem Hadar said. "I was instructed only to deliver terms."

Terms—a strange reference from the Vorta. Terms for surrender or terms for a treaty?

"I see. . . . Well, then I want to talk to someone who can negotiate. I want to speak with your First."

The Jem Hadar soldier paused, shifted his feet uneasily, eyed Sisko as if he didn't know exactly how to respond to that.

After a moment he said, "There is no First."

Sisko measured the soldier's reaction. "I take it there's no Second either."

"I command the unit," the soldier admitted.

In those few words a flood of active possibilities rushed into Sisko's mind. There was a problem in the Jem Hadar camp. They had crashed. Their Vorta was injured, and this soldier, the Third, was in command, but he hadn't been promoted to first or even second, and that meant he must've done something wrong. He didn't deserve the posting, even though he had the job. That meant tension between him and the other Jem Hadar who also could not move up until he did, and it meant some kind of tug and pull was going on between him and the Vorta.

Hmm. . . .

"It must be hard," Sisko prodded, "for a soldier to take orders from a Vorta."

The soldier stiffened. "The Vorta command the Jem Hadar. It is the order of things."

"'Obedience brings victory,'" Sisko recited, and got a strong surprised look from the soldier. "I was on a mission with the Jem Hadar once, before the war, of course. They were good . . . tough. Professional. It was an honor to serve with them. But their Vorta . . . he was something different. Manipulative. Treacherous. Trusted by neither side. In the end, he was killed . . . by the Jem Hadar First."

The Third blinked and gaped, unable to hide his shock.

"Surprised?" Sisko asked quietly.

Nervous but fighting to recover, the Third fidgeted.

"Such things have been known to happen, but they are rare and only occur in units that have lost discipline." He paused then, twitching under Sisko's analytical glare, then forced back the subject he'd come here about. "The Vorta has instructed me to give you his assurance that neither you nor the doctor will be harmed and you'll both be free to leave at the end of your meeting. What is your response?"

"The Vorta's word doesn't carry much weight with me," Sisko snapped. "Can I have *your* assurance that we'll be free to go, Remata'Klan?"

Moved by the unexpected faith from an enemy who pointedly did not take the Vorta as superior, the Third hesitated and searched around for an answer that wouldn't compromise the loyalty he was supposed to hold for the Vorta.

"I have been ordered," he said slowly, "to let you leave after the meeting. You can be sure that I will obey that order."

Sisko paused a couple of seconds, just to imply that none of this meant quite as much to him as it did to the Jem Hadar, but then said, "We'll make the trade in one hour."

"Agreed."

Remata'Klan turned and boiled out of the cavern with new things to think about.

When the footsteps faded and he and Dax were alone, she opened her eyes.

"Sounded like you were actually getting through to him for a minute there."

Sisko shook his head. "You can't break through all that Dominion conditioning in one conversation."

"Do you really think you can turn him against his Vorta?"

"I don't know. But there were at least seven Jem Hadar soldiers up on that ridge this morning. Say at least two more at their base camp, guarding the Vorta and their prisoners. Without Nog and Garak on our side, that gives them almost a two to one advantage."

Grimly, Dax blinked and sighed. "I think I'd like to check out now."

"So would I, old man, so would I."

"Don't trust them, Benjamin," she said, letting the concern rise in her weakened voice.

"I don't," he told her, "but if they've got Garak and Nog, I have to do something. I have the moral and legal authority to sacrifice myself for them as their commanding officer—"

"But that doesn't include Julian."

"Better him that Nog, at least."

"True. . . ."

"Sisko to Bashir."

"Bashir, sir."

"Doctor, come back to the cavern. I have something to tell you."

The rain it raineth on the just,
And also on the unjust fella:
But chiefly on the just, because
The unjust steals the just's umbrella.

Lord Bowen

CHAPTER
14

KIRA NERYS stood at the rail overlooking the Promenade of *Deep Space Nine*. Below, a flow of people moved like a sleepy beast. Jem Hadar soldiers, a couple of Vorta, Cardassians, assorted other aliens, and now Bajorans who had returned to the station or were visiting. All was quiet—rather too quiet. There was function here, but no joy. There was life, but it possessed no bubble. The taste of her morning's raktajino lingered on her lips, growing stale. Lingering in her mind, unerasable, the image of Jem Hadar and Cardassians manning the posts in Ops, posts which only weeks ago had been home to the friendly faces of Dax, O'Brien, and her other friends.

Friends. . . .

Day by day she had taken raktajino from Mavek every morning. She had gone about her daily routine.

She had resisted any efforts to fight back against the Cardassian occupation, clinging to the glimmer of hope that Captain Sisko was out there somewhere, with a plan to take the station back, or at least a plan in which Kira's patience played a part. Even pressure from Vedek Kassim, one of Bajor's most prominent religious leaders, had not moved Kira to accept her one-time role as a rebel troublemaker. This business of a command position had been hard to understand at first, but she had acclimated, learned to comprehend the balancing act every officer must employ, and now it was her job not only to avoid making trouble herself, but to see that trouble was not made by others.

Thus her shame when, just hours ago, Vedek Kassim threw herself from this very rail to her death at the flat walkway of the Promenade. Her heart half eaten away, Kira looked down and knew the Vedek's desperation had been caused by Kira's own resistance to . . . resistance. The Vedek's sacrifice, and her final cry—*"Evil must be opposed!"*—was a message as much for Kira as for the Dominion and the Cardassians.

Despite appearances, there had been some unsavory changes that even Captain Sisko didn't know about since Bajor had been completely cut off from outside trade. Because of the Vedek's suicide, Gul Dukat had initiated a crackdown on security.

On top of all that, four hundred Dominion facilitators had been sent to Bajor to "help" because of all the shortages they had themselves caused with the isolation policy. Technical assistance for a few months. Sure.

Kira herself and Odo had welcomed a group of Vorta to the station. That was part of their duty under the damned treaty with Bajor. That made it seem that Odo, supposedly a "Founder," was validating the Dominion's presence, especially now that he had accepted a position, in a deal with Weyoun, on the "ruling council" of the station. Odo had made a request, and Weyoun had cleverly turned it around on him. Now Odo appeared, in the eyes of all here, to be approving of the Dominion and Cardassian rule. Kira downright knew she was validating it just by not fighting it. Sickening.

And all this was further irritated by Jake Sisko's new habit of lurking about, playing the part of an investigative reporter. . . . That's all they needed. Freedom of the press didn't exist in a totalitarian state, kid, and it can work against freedom when the press doesn't know better than to keep its mouth shut.

Over and over Kira heard the words of Vedek Kassim trying to convince her to rise against the Dominion. *"The Prophets tell us that evil must be opposed. The Dominion is evil. . . . As Bajor's liaison officer, what will you do to oppose them? . . . Freedoms are being curtailed one by one. . . . Can't you see what's happening to you? You're becoming an apologist for them. . . ."*

Kira vaguely recalled her response—not to apologize for the Dominion, but a warning to Vedek Kassim that any public protest would have to be stopped and it was Kira's job to stop it. What would it have taken to—

"Nerys?"

She almost turned, guarding a flinch at the interruption, but then recognized Odo's voice and didn't need to turn. Her eyes were still fixed upon the scuffed floor down below where Vedek Kassim had lay dead before her, before everyone. Pedestrians below were deliberately avoiding even walking over the spot.

"Damar has been trying to contact you for the past five hours," he said, coming to her side at the rail.

Silently Kira opened her hand and showed her unactivated combadge, then closed her fist again. No explanation for that.

"I keep thinking about it," she murmured. "Over and over . . . and I just can't believe that I stood down there, ready to use force to stop a protest against the Dominion. *Me!* When I was in the Resistance . . . I despised people like me. I'm a collaborator, Odo. . . ."

"That's not true." His gravelly voice was calm, without pressure. "You're doing exactly what Captain Sisko wanted you and the rest of Bajor to do—remain neutral and stay out of the fighting."

"We used to have a saying in the Resistance," she told him with a touch of reverie. " 'If you're not fighting them, you're helping them.' Half the Alpha Quadrant is out there right now, fighting for freedom. But not me. . . . How do I spend my time? I get a full meal every day, I sleep in a soft bed every night, I even write reports for the murderers who run this station—"

Odo cut her off. "This is a difficult time for everyone. Do you think it's easy for me to sit down with Dukat and Weyoun every day while they plot the destruction of the Federation?"

Now she looked at him. "I'm not pointing a finger at you, Odo. I'm the one who told you to get more involved in the first place. No, this is about me . . . this is about being able to look in the mirror every morning and not feel nauseated by what I see. Kassim was right. . . . I've got to do something. I've got to start fighting back."

"That's a mistake," he said. "Active resistance will trigger a crackdown and—"

"Odo, I don't want to end up fighting you, too, but I'll do it if I have to."

There was a quiet pause between them now. She hadn't had to put much inflection into her words—the conviction behind them carried perfectly well to the perceptions of her longtime friend.

And to Odo's credit, he wasn't foolish enough to argue. But even more, Kira sensed that he too had been wallowing in his own personal disgusts.

He glanced about, then lowered his voice. "All right. But let's find a more discreet place to plan the New Resistance."

"The next thing we need is a secure way to communicate with our contacts on Bajor."

"The Cardassians are extremely adept at locating the source of any illicit subspace transmission."

"Then we'll have to be smarter than they are."

Kira made her cryptic declaration almost flippantly. She and Odo sat alone in Quark's bar, in the middle of a jumble of activity and the rattle of the Dabo wheel that masked their conversation. Nobody would expect a resistance cell to be meeting in the most crowded place on the station. Everybody knew she and Odo were friends. No one expected them to avoid each other. So it was perfect to talk here, plot and plan here, consider here, worry here.

"Hi. Mind if I join in?"

Kira straightened a little as the lanky Jake Sisko made a predictable appearance. Here to ask lots of questions, write them down, try to get them spread around, make a name for himself doing it. Just what every resistance cell needed.

"You already have," Odo droned.

The boy—all right, he wasn't a boy anymore, except for that silly glitter in his eyes—leaned on both elbows and flatly said, "I want in."

Kira glanced at Odo, and he returned that same troubled look.

"In on what?" Odo asked.

"Your resistance cell."

They hadn't even done anything yet! How could he possibly know? Were they *that* rusty?

Managing to bury a groan of frustration, Kira tossed off, "What cell?"

"Come on, Major, I have my sources."

Odo shifted in his chair and leered at Kira. "How reassuring."

She knew exactly what he meant. She also knew that neither she nor Odo had said anything to anybody. How had Jake found out about their embryonic resistance?

"I can help," Jake attempted.

"How?"

"As a reporter, I hear things. People talk to me."

Ridiculous—nobody who wanted anything kept private would talk to him, so who cared to hear about anything from anybody who *would* talk to Jake Sisko?

Kira evasively asked, "About what?"

"Major," he said with a twinge of protest, "all I'm asking for is a chance."

Irritation burned under Kira's skin, but she was saved from any response when Quark showed up and with typical rudeness interrupted them. "It's time, Major."

Well, after all, she'd asked him to do this. "Already?" she sighed.

"Fourteen hundred fifty-seven hours. The shuttle will be docking in three minutes."

Resigned, and yet also glad to be leaving Jake behind, Kira got up. "I better go," she said with unshielded sarcasm. "I wouldn't want to keep him waiting."

Leaving Jake to stew in his own choice of careers, she left the bar, and was gratified when Odo followed her out. It was a clear message to Jake that, if they were indeed doing something subversive, he couldn't be part of it. Not yet, anyway. Son of the emissary or not.

Kira held back on the Promenade until Odo caught up with her.

"How did he know?" she huffed. "Do you think Quark talked?"

Odo glanced back, to make sure Jake was not following. "No, I don't think he would. It's quite possible that Jake is making a logical conclusion based upon his familiarity with us. After the Vedek's suicide, it's not a far-fetched idea that you might have been pushed too far. It's possible Jake was only acting upon supposition."

"Pretty good supposition. . . . That's all we need— to be that predictable. I wonder if Dukat or Weyoun are having the same suspicions."

"Dukat hasn't been on the station for days."

"Don't remind me. He and Damar practically danced for joy when they left to organize the Dominion facilitators on Bajor. They actually asked me to go with them! Can you imagine?"

"Doesn't matter for now whether or not they suspect us of activity. We haven't done anything yet. All we have to do is nothing for a few more days—or at least, nothing that looks as if it could be the work of a resistance coalition."

"I hate having to go meet them in the airlock, as if they were *somebody.* . . ."

Odo paused before going off in another direction— his presence wasn't required and might be misread at the airlock. "Keep in mind, Nerys, that anything you do to placate them can from now on work in our favor. Relax, and they will relax also."

With a dirty little smile, Kira shook her head and leered at him. "Quit being so wise. It makes me feel inferior."

He returned a very small ironic smile, and veered off. Wise again—they wanted to be seen together, but no more than usual.

The walk to the airlock was mind clearing, though without comfort and left her physically chilled. This was her job, yes, but Odo was right—somehow this ceremonial crap would ultimately help her to be effective as a revolutionary. The authority would come into play . . . eventually. It had to, or it would drive her crazy.

The airlock rolled open less than a full second after she arrived. Gul Dukat strolled out already bearing a beam to beam smile, and behind him, with an equally poignant and venomous glare, was Glinn Damar.

"Major Kira," Dukat greeted, "so good to see you again."

But Damar was less formal. "You're out of uniform, Major. Bajorans could use a lesson in respect."

"Damar, please," Dukat said. "This is a happy occasion. Let's not spoil it. Major, I have a surprise for you."

"Nerys!"

Kira turned at the sound of her name being called from the airlock.

"Nerys, I'm so glad to see you!"

A buoyant young woman shot from the airlock and clasped Kira in a bear hug.

"Ziyal—what are you doing here?"

Kira drew back to get a good look at the girl's face, chalky and gray as a Cardassian's, obviously the dominant race in her heritage, but she also had that touch of Bajoran construction that showed at the bridge of her nose. Dukat's daughter—Dukat and a Bajoran slave. . . .

"You're supposed to be on Bajor," Kira told her.

Dukat beamed at them. "I talked her into taking a little sabbatical from the university."

Kira leered at him. *You* talked her into it?

"It didn't take much convincing," Ziyal admitted joyously. "Why don't you and I have dinner tonight? I'll tell you all about it."

"All right. . . ."

"Splendid!" Dukat clasped his hands. "We'll dine in my quarters at twenty-two hundred."

"What a minute! That's not what I—"

But Ziyal cut her off and grasped her by both hands. "I can't tell you how much I've missed you!"

Before Kira had a chance to protest again, Dukat strode away down the corridor and tossed back, "Come along, Ziyal."

Ziyal rushed off after her father, but called back to Kira, "See you tonight!"

"I'm not having dinner with you tonight. I'm *not* having dinner with you tonight. . . . I'm sorry, but I'm just not going to be able to have dinner with you tonight. I'm *not* really sorry, it's just a matter of principle, I hope you understand, but I won't be having dinner with you tonight or any night, or any year, or at least not until I shoot my head off. Oh, shut up and ring the stupid door chime."

"Come in," Ziyal called from the other side of the door.

Kira walked in, unable to hide her tension.

"Nerys!" Ziyal was finishing setting the table with Dukat's finest crystal and flatware. "You're early! I just started the ramufta."

Kira crossed the room to the table. "Ziyal, I'm not having dinner with you tonight."

Ziyal paused, but her expression showed that this wasn't entirely unexpected. "Oh. . . . It's because of my father, isn't it?"

"That's right."

"I thought you might back out. . . . I was hoping I was wrong." Ziyal bothered to straighten a salad fork, but made no effort to hide her disappointment.

"Ziyal," Kira began, "what are you doing back on the station?"

"Please don't be upset with me," the girl said. "I know how hard you worked to arrange things for me on Bajor. I tried—I really tried."

"I'm not upset with you. Just a little confused. Now tell me what happened."

"It wasn't any one thing. . . . The students at the university, everybody was . . . polite. But I'd see them whispering in the hallways and staring at me. I'm the daughter of Gul Dukat. My father is leading a war against the emissary of the Prophets. I don't know what made me think I could fit in."

She sank heavily to the couch, engulfed in the minute painful hits a young person could get from a situation that others might see as frivolous.

Not quite unfeeling about this, Kira sat next to her, but had no words of comfort to offer. This wasn't much of a time for comfort, not as much as for reality. Ziyal's return to the station made Kira's job that much harder. If she were to involve herself with a resistance movement, make life on the station more hazardous, more risky, then she would have to accept that Ziyal, a person about whom she deeply cared, might be caught in the cross fire.

"This station," Ziyal murmured, "is the closest thing to a home that I have. You're here. . . . My father's here—"

"And the last time you defied him," Kira harshly reminded, "he left you here to die."

"We talked about that." Ziyal turned a plaintive gaze to her. "He admits he overreacted, but family loyalty is important to my father and he felt I betrayed him."

"*You* betrayed *him?* I think it's the other way around."

"He misses me, Nerys . . . and I've missed him."

Scratched by the sudden warmth between father and daughter, Kira pushed to her feet and walked to the viewport to regain control over her expression.

"I have to give him a chance," Ziyal said behind her. "He's all I have, except for you. I was hoping you'd have dinner with us tonight, because there's something special I wanted to share with both of you . . . but I guess that's impossible."

Her insides churning, Kira wanted very much to declare an assault on Ziyal for siding with her father and detach herself from this odd family relationship the three of them seemed to have. Looking at Ziyal, at the girl's downcast eyes, the smear of her hopes, Kira couldn't spit the venom at Ziyal that was meant for Dukat.

"All right," she conceded. "I'll be here. But I can't guarantee it's going to be much fun."

Ziyal hesitated, looked at her, then jumped to her feet as joy spread across her face. "I promise my father will behave!"

A flower. Actually, a pretty well executed minimalist monochrome ink brush evocation of a single Bajoran lily pushing up out of the barren rocks of Nocroma Bayside. This and several others of Ziyal's artwork were laid out on the coffee table. Kira now wore her dress uniform, and so Dukat also was wearing his.

Dinner had been cordial but stiff. The conduit had been Ziyal, who loved them both, and Kira and Dukat had both been making a true effort to make her happy, suspending their mutual tension. Kira had more to suspend than Dukat. Kira knew he'd always been interested in her, first as an enemy, later as a . . . let's call it a gaming opponent, and more recently as a woman—what a joke. All this made Kira uneasy, but somehow she had been on this station, among Cardassians on a working plane, for a long time now and had found variety in herself that she never expected. She'd spent the evening, for Ziyal's sake, looking for distractions. First, the spacescape out the viewport. Then the dinner itself. The decapus salad. A little tough, but spiced right. The main course. A little bland, but wonderfully tender. After dinner, drinks. Now, Ziyal's artwork provided some conversation, a further reason to avoid any touchy subjects—and to Kira's pleasure, the art really was very moving and Ziyal had good news to go with it.

"The Institute is having an exhibition of new artists next month and the director might want to include my work," Ziyal bubbled. "It's a chance to show that both Bajorans and Cardassians look at the universe the same way. That's what I want to do with my work . . . bring people together."

Breathless, Ziyal stopped herself, suddenly aware of how she sounded, and Kira hoped it was not her own patronizing expression that Ziyal had noticed.

"I guess that sounds a little silly," the girl diminished.

Dukat puffed up and proclaimed, "On the contrary, my dear, you're quite eloquent."

Kira was glad Dukat spoke up. She didn't want to laud Ziyal for a simplistic hope, but that's what it was. Artwork, or any manner of passive inoculation, simply couldn't bring people together who had fundamental moral differences. Struggle, disagreement, and conflict were, at their core, healthy elements of society—at least, a free society. If everybody just got along and bottled up their disagreements . . . well, you could find yourself sitting on a couch with a despot and smiling the whole time. And the despot would win.

"Are you ready for dessert?" Ziyal stood up, not waiting for an answer.

"I'm not going anywhere," Kira offered as the girl scampered off toward the galley, seeming very young.

Alone on the couch with Dukat, Kira kept looking at the artwork. "I don't believe the change. I've never seen her so—"

"Happy?" the Cardassian imperial leader filled in. "Neither have I, Major."

"She's finally found something. A talent, a direction."

"I'm reluctant to admit it, but you were right to send her to Bajor," Dukat offered.

"I'm glad it worked out."

He leaned back, crossed his legs, sipped his drink, and looked at her. "We seldom see eye-to-eye, Major, but I know you care about my daughter . . . and for that I'm grateful."

His gratitude ran like chills up Kira's arms, yet she wasn't inclined to deny its veracity. That was odd—but instinctive. Something told her he wasn't playing any games right now. The gaze he had given Ziyal as she dashed away—real pride.

"Ziyal's excited by all this," Kira told him, with a tone that offered a hand of cooperation for now. "A chance to have her work on exhibit? What an accomplishment."

"I'm hosting a celebration for her in my quarters. I hope you'll join me."

"When?"

"Twenty-one-thirty tomorrow. Unless I'm unavoidably delayed."

Kira leaned back. "The busy life of an interstellar despot."

"I prefer the term 'tyrant.'"

Kira smiled, and a good mood started creeping over her hesitations. Dukat was throwing her a bone, seeming to understand for once what it was like to be on the receiving side of oppression.

"I was thinking," he went on, "of assigning Damar to escort Ziyal to the affair."

"Damar? You can't be serious!"

"He's a fine officer from a good family."

Kira huffed. "He's a self-righteous sycophant who despises everything Bajoran."

"I assure you, Major," Dukat attempted, "Damar doesn't despise your people."

"Then why does his upper lip curl every time he says the word 'Bajor'?" She curled her own lip, bared her teeth, and mimicked, "'Bajorans could use a lesson in respect.'"

Dukat narrowed his eyes. "He does no such thing—"

The door chimed and without waiting for a call, the panel opened. Damar strode in, and Kira quickly put her lip back in place, wondering if he were not part Betazoid and could read minds.

"Gul Dukat?" Damar approached his leader with a padd.

"Ah, Damar . . . impeccable timing, as always." Dukat glanced at Kira with a light in his eye.

Kira pressed her lips flat, trying not to laugh.

"Sir," Damar said, "the *Bajoran* delegation requests that the replicators be shipped by *Bajoran* transports."

Oh, damn—the laugh broke out. She tried not to look at Damar, although it indeed seemed ridiculous that she was laughing at the pictures of flowers. Oh, who really cared what Damar thought?

"Thank you, Damar," she spoke up, taking the role of the Bajoran authority in the middle of this joke. "That will be all."

Damar glowered at her and parted his lips to snarl back, but Dukat interrupted. "You heard the major."

"Sir?"

Holding a breath, Dukat insisted. "We'll continue this discussion another time."

Drawing himself up, Damar acceded. "Very well."

He executed an about-face and strode out of the quarters.

Kira held her own breath. Dukat looked at the door for several seconds, but finally had to meet Kira's eyes. "I believe I owe you an apology," he said. "You and . . . the *Bajoran* people."

His teeth showed and his lips peeled back.

Together, the two of them dissolved into laughter. Something in common. Something at last.

In common. . . .

"I have something for you." Dukat stood up and drew a box from behind the chair near the viewport. "A gift. For the party."

"Oh. . . ." Carrying the box to the table, she opened it.

A long silky gown tumbled over her arms, shimmering with fine crushed gems embedded right into the stretchy fabric.

"Oh," she murmured again, and held the gown up against her body. It was the perfect length, a little revealing, soft and luscious, flowing and tempting.

Moving to a mirror next to the door panel, Kira gazed at the vision of herself with the beautiful gown drifting across her form.

A soldier in a dancing dress . . . out of place, somehow . . . out of . . .

Disgust creased her brow. "What the hell am I doing?"

From near the couch, Dukat said, "Pardon?"

Suddenly boiling, Kira swung around and dumped the dress back into the box. The shimmering fabric spilled into its container, virtually folding itself, and still looked beautiful just lying there.

"You don't like the dress?" Dukat asked.

"The dress is fine." She turned to face him. "I don't like you."

"Major, that's just not true," he said, disturbingly genuine. "There's a bond between us—"

"Only in your mind. You're an opportunistic, power-hungry dictator and I want nothing to do with you."

Pausing a moment, Dukat seemed sincerely disappointed, which only made Kira feel worse.

"Ziyal will be disappointed to hear you say that," he told her.

"She'll get over it."

"Nerys," Dukat attempted, "why don't we sit down and talk about this."

Get out. Get out quickly. Let him make any excuse to Ziyal that he could come up with. Let him explain to his daughter that her mother was a slave of Cardassian masters and that was why she felt so ill at ease with Bajorans or Cardassians alike. Let him tell her that her dear friend and mentor Nerys was not a de-facto mother, but in reality was a trapped enemy whose life of hunger and deprivation had once been devoted to repelling the occupation of despots.

Sit down and talk about it?

"No," she snapped. "No, we won't."

Theirs not to make reply,
Theirs not to reason why,
Theirs but to do or die.

CHAPTER

15

"ARE YOU TWO all right?"

"Perfect. How are you?"

"I've felt better."

Good enough for now. Sisko and Bashir kept walking after exchanging only those little words with Nog and Garak. They didn't even break stride as they passed each other on the stretch of sand, Garak and Nog heading for the Starfleet cluster at one end of the beach, Sisko and Bashir heading for the stand of Jem Hadar at the other. Bashir carried only his medikit. Sisko carried nothing. That was the deal.

Remata'Klan was here. Another Jem Hadar, probably the fourth, introduced himself as Limara'Son. They walked straight—absolutely straight—to a cavern on another part of the beach, chilling Sisko with awareness of how close the two camps really were.

Inside the cave were other Jem Hadar soldiers, watching warily and fingering their weapons and twitching uneasily as Sisko and Bashir were led to the makeshift resting place of a very ill Vorta. Bashir immediately knelt at the Vorta's side, but the Vorta had no attention for the doctor. Instead he eyed Sisko with his penetrating gaze.

"Captain Sisko," he said weakly, "my name is Keevan. We have a lot to talk about."

"Not for a while, you don't," Bashir contradicted, and looked up at Sisko. "He needs immediate surgery."

"Now?" Sisko asked.

"I don't have any choice."

Well, that was an honest answer. Sisko could tell from Bashir's tone that the doctor wasn't bluffing and had a genuine patient on his hands and that his Hippocratic oath had just kicked in, enemy or not.

Apparently the Jem Hadar also picked up the snap of urgency in Bashir's voice, for they suddenly clustered closer.

Bashir looked up, intimidated. "I'm a doctor—I won't hurt him."

The Vorta smiled. "They're not here to protect me. They've just never seen what the inside of a Vorta looks like."

Curious—Jem Hadar soldiers crowding around to see the guts of a being they thought was somehow closer to the gods.

On the other hand, Sisko wasn't interested in a good look, and stepped aside to let the Jem Hadar provide a convenient screen. Bashir went to work in studious silence. The Vorta must have been only minutes from death.

Sisko beat down feelings of just letting the posturing alien die, but that would leave the Jem Hadar without guidance and he thought he could more easily deal with a Vorta who owed him one than an uncontrolled pawn who didn't and who was going through withdrawal.

Yes, he decided, they must be short on ketracel white. These Jem Hadar were twitching and nervous, eyeing each other suspiciously, perhaps experiencing the first signs of mental instability which would soon lead to collapse if they weren't "fed."

The surgery took a while. Sisko was from time to time tempted to take a peek. The Vorta must be very complex inside for Bashir to take so long, either that or the injuries were multiple and scattered. Halfway through, Bashir's jacket came off and an IV went in.

After—must have been at least two hours, for Sisko had no way to tell the time—Bashir let out a relieved sigh and stood up. When the Jem Hadar parted and moved off, Sisko could see the Vorta with his chest bandaged, still hooked up to the IV.

"How was the show?" Sisko asked as Remata'Klan approached him.

"Informative."

The noncommittal answer was flat and pointless, but the Jem Hadar officer's face looked like a spooked cow's. Sisko was about to comment when the Vorta stirred.

"I . . . am . . . alive. . . ."

Bashir gazed down at his patient as he cleaned his hands, then picked up his tricorder. "No self-diagnoses, please. I'm the doctor here. Internal hemorrhaging has stopped. . . . Your free collagen levels are dropping. . . . Tissue growth factors have stabilized. . . . And there's a fifty percent rise in cell oxygenation. You're alive. Be careful—most of your insides are being held together with cellular microsutures and a lot of hope."

With the warning that motion could unpin him like a fabric pattern, the Vorta stopped trying to shift his position. "Leave us," he told Remata'Klan, and motioned to the Jem Hadar. "And take them with you."

Once they were gone, Keevan pointed at a black case. "May I have that, please?" he asked Bashir.

With a glance for permission toward Sisko, Bashir obliged him.

Keevan worked the security lock on the case. "There are ten Jem Hadar soldiers on this planet, Captain."

He opened the case and displayed the interior. A ketracel white storage and distribution case—except that the case was smeared with crushed glass and spilled white. Some had been distributed. The rest—all the remaining tubes of ketracel white had been smashed except for one last vial.

"That," the Vorta went on, "is the only vial of ketracel white we have left. When it's gone, my hold over them will be broken. They'll become nothing more than senseless, violent animals. And they'll kill anyone they can—you, me, and the rest of your men. And finally they will turn on each other."

"Why are you telling us this?" Sisko demanded, cutting to the bottom line.

Keevan let his head fall back and seemed to realize Sisko was growing impatient. "I'm going to order the Jem Hadar to attack your base camp in the morning. But I will provide you with their precise plan of attack. You should be able to kill them all."

Expediency was one thing, but this . . . Sisko stared at him. "They're your own men!"

"Yes."

"You still haven't answered my question. Why are you doing this?"

Keeven gestured to communication gear on the other side of the cavern. "That's a communication system. It needs repair, but I'm willing to bet you've brought one of those famed Starfleet engineers who can turn rocks into replicators. He should have a lot more success repairing it that a Jem Hadar suffering from withdrawal."

Sisko and Bashir both looked at the communication system, trying not to gaze too hungrily, but Sisko realized they were poorly hiding their temptation.

"After you take care of the Jem Hadar," Keevan went on, "I'll give you the comm system and surrender to you as a prisoner of war."

Bashir cast him an unfriendly glance. "And you spend the rest of the war resting comfortably as a Starfleet POW while your men lie rotting on this planet."

Turning his head to look at the man who had just

saved his life, Keevan made no apologies. The Jem Hadar were doomed, if this was all the white left, that was true enough. It was down to him or them, and they were dead already.

"I see we understand each other," Keevan rasped. "I'm ordering the Jem Hadar to attack your position tomorrow whether you agree to my terms or not. So you can either kill them or they'll kill you. Either way, they're coming."

Distasteful, but certainly effective. Keevan had assessed the situation about as razor-sharply as could be asked. He was acting upon his best interest, as anyone else would do, but somehow there was a cold ball of heartlessness at the bottom of this. Perhaps it was the lack of regret that plucked so sour a string.

He had the Jem Hadar figured out, and unfortunately he had Sisko figured out too. Sisko was backed into a corner. Use the information or don't use it. Cooperate or don't. The Jem Hadar were coming.

Standing here in the wake of the ultimatum, Sisko felt like a perfect fool. Out there in the bay was a shipload of ketracel white, at the bottom of the sea. When he'd seen the Jem Hadar spiraling in, why hadn't he thought to salvage a case of the stuff? What a bargaining chip it would've given him!

Instead, he stood there with his hands empty and little to do but play into the Vorta's struggle to survive.

As he and Bashir stood there not liking any of this, the Vorta quietly began to draw a diagram in the sand.

"This is your base camp. . . . Two kilometers to the

south is a canyon. I will order the Jem Hadar to follow the canyon floor . . ."

"What are they talking about with the Star-fleeters?"

"I don't know. It's not for me to know. Or you."

Limara'Son. "The Vorta will betray us now that his life is saved."

Troubling thoughts. Betrayed, distrust. Ugly to a mind conditioned to believe.

Remata'Klan. "He will live."

"We should have let him die. Then we could open the case and get the white and live ourselves. Now, our lives are in his hands."

"Our lives were always in his hands."

"But now the Starfleeters are of more value to him than we are. There are ten of us and we are starving. When the Vorta needed us to keep him alive, we had an advantage. We have no advantages now. We have nothing to offer him. The Starfleeters have a doctor and food for him."

Remata'Klan, disturbed. "What would you have me do? Or what should I have done before?"

Limara'Son. A pause. "You saved me from the Vorta's rage. He could've ordered me destroyed for what I did."

"You did not disobey orders. You were overcome by the hunger. I have trouble understanding what a Jem Hadar is supposed to do when two forces pull upon the inner will. What is expected of us? How do others resolve the struggle?"

"Humans handle such trouble." Limara'Son. "They seem to thrive on the struggle inside."

He also didn't understand, apparently.

"Why won't the Vorta give us white?" Limara'Son. "Now that he will live, he should make sure we will live also. He has the same obligation to us that we have to him."

Remata'Klan. "We all serve the Dominion as a working unit. Together, we move forward."

"Except that we have one leg now, and the Vorta is in charge of that. I have never known such . . . such . . ."

"Nor have I. What would you do, if you were First?"

"Or Third?"

"Yes . . . or Third."

"Attack the Starfleet encampment. Kill them all. The Vorta will be forced to deal with us."

"That is against obedience."

"Shall we have obedience or shall we have survival, Remata'Klan? We can have no obedience to anything if we fail to survive. Is it not our duty to survive in order to continue serving the Dominion?"

Remata'Klan . . . inner quake. "And if the Vorta fails to help us survive, then he has stopped serving the Dominion. I do not know anymore what to do . . . how to choose. There must be a manner of obedience that does not involve treason."

"But if the Vorta is treasonous, if he is dealing with the Federation for his own survival, then it becomes our obligation to—"

"Enough, Limara'Son. This is destructive talk."

"Is it? Then here is more. . . . I believe the Vorta has no more white."

A piercing terror. No white? Shuddering hands, frozen legs. Remata'Klan. "Why would he say he did?"

"To keep us in his control, to keep us doing his bidding until he can deal with Starfleet and get them to save him from this place."

Arguments pressing on the mind. . . . Weakness spawns a cloying trouble of thoughts that are all naughty.

This guilt . . . ugly and purposeless.

Limara'Son. "Now they have saved his life. He has no need of us."

"These thoughts . . ." Remata'Klan. ". . . are bad for Jem Hadar. These kinds of thoughts make us too much like them. We can't be like them, Limara'Son. . . . We have to remain Jem Hadar, or all begins to dissolve. No one will fear us anymore. The Dominion will lose the war."

Limara'Son's gaze. "All this lies upon you and me? Our unit?"

"Yes. All this is on us now. What we do, everyone will hear. The Dominion, the Jem Hadar, the Cardassians, the Federation. . . . There will be no one who respects Jem Hadar anymore if you and I fail to obey in the face of betrayal. Ours is not to set precedents. We must not carve new ways. If the Vorta betrays us, the indignity is his, not ours. The reports will say that the Vorta lied, the Vorta cheated, the Vorta betrayed, but the Jem Hadar obeyed to the end and stood strong in our vow. Our lives are worth that, Limara'Son . . .

so the Jem Hadar can be higher than the Vorta in the eyes of everyone . . . just one time."

". . . and once they've reached this point, we'll have them in a cross fire."

Ben Sisko's officers glowered over the sand diagram he had just re-created on their own cave floor. He felt like some kind of stooge.

"They won't have a chance," Ensign Gordon observed.

"That's the idea," Garak told him. "In case you've forgotten, we're in a war and they're the enemy."

"There are rules, Garak," O'Brien sourly commented, "even in war."

"Correction," the Cardassian smart-mouthed. "Humans have rules in war. Rules that tend to make victory a little harder to achieve, in my opinion."

"So we just shoot them down?"

Sisko let them wrangle. He didn't want to get in on it. They could make any excuses or complaints they wanted, but he knew the truth. They were being used by the Vorta for his own survival. Keevan was giving them an advantage they dared not turn down, and that was more distasteful than a supposed officer setting up his own men, even if they were going to die anyway.

When Nog issued a protest, though, that was too much. Sisko snapped, "This isn't a vote. The decision's mine. And Garak's right—we're at war. Given a choice between us or them, there is no choice. Let's move out."

They scooped up their weapons and hurried out

rather faster than they had to, anxious to put this bitter episode behind them, leaving Sisko to linger a moment with Dax. If things went badly and the Starfleet team was all killed, she would be here alone, injured, on a planet with a recovering Vorta and whichever of the withdrawing Jem Hadar were left over.

"I'd say good luck," Dax uttered, "but I don't think you'll need it."

Sisko bottled a temptation to growl something about having a desperate Vorta on their side instead of luck, but he didn't need that any more than she did. "Say it anyway. Because I'm still hoping there's another way out of this."

"In that case," she offered, "good luck, Benjamin."

With a short nod and a wish to stay, he simply turned his back on her and hurried out after his crew. She knew the realities as well as he did. No sense prolonging the painful.

The blood-red sun was now rising over the horizon. The small planet's single ocean made an uneasy mirror, with one distant island lying upon it like a pumpkin seed.

The two muscles of rock which held the two caverns and the two base camps came together on the other side of the ridge into a box canyon, a narrow passage with high walls on either side—textbook recipe for ambush. From a precipice, Sisko and his crew watched as Remata'Klan and Limara'Son traveled down through the passage with the rest of their men. Even from here, even in this early light, the twitching of their limbs, the shaking of their heads, the trembling of their hands was obvious. Withdrawal was taking its toll on them already. Soon they would lose what was left of their self-control and go mad with need. Already they were having trouble concentrating, focusing on the path, keeping in line.

Remata'Klan kept glancing at his men. He knew what would come if they failed.

Sisko had no idea what the Vorta had told them— probably that the Starfleet crew had some stores of white in that ship. Strange how close to right he was, if that was his story. It had to be his story—what else could he have told ten hungry Jem Hadar in order to make them do something this profoundly untactical?

All the Starfleeters had to do was open fire. . . . All they had to do was mow down the enemy who were clustered now into a perfect target.

Fire.

Ready. . . . Fire.

Aim. Fire. Phasers fire. All hands . . .

Sisko shook his head. The order froze on his tongue.

He stood up abruptly, surprising even himself.

"Remata'Klan!"

The Jem Hadar all whirled, and spotted him as he stood tall above them from an obviously stronger position.

"I want to talk!" he shouted.

Remata'Klan paused, measured the situation, then called back, "Agreed!"

The soldier then said something to his men, and left them behind to walk toward Sisko.

Sisko left his astonished crew behind and picked his

way down the ridge to meet the Third halfway. They stopped several paces apart.

"There's no way out of this canyon," Sisko said, "and we have phaser locks on every one of you."

Remata'Klan glanced around the canyon. He didn't need convincing. "You appear to have a decisive advantage."

"A battle under these circumstances would serve no purpose. I'm prepared to offer you terms—hear me out! I know that you need more ketracel white. My doctor can sedate your men and keep them alive until we're rescued. After that, we can put you into medical stasis until we secure a new supply."

Remata'Klan shook his big rocky head. "The Vorta did not give me the option to surrender."

"Keevan's betrayed you." With that, Sisko laid every card he had on the table, short of telling the Jem Hadar that a shipload of ketracel white lay a deep dive away. That far . . . he would not go. Instead, he finished, "He gave us your entire plan of attack last night."

Remata'Klan wasn't as moved by the news as Sisko expected. "It was obvious that approaching your position through this canyon was a deliberate tactical error on his part."

Now it was Sisko's turn to pause. "You knew?"

"I suspected. Despite what Keevan may think, the Jem Hadar are often one step ahead of the Vorta."

"You can stay one step ahead. Surrender."

"I have my orders."

"He hasn't earned the unwavering loyalty you're giving him," Sisko said honestly. "He's a manipulative little creature trying to save his own neck by sacrificing you and your men."

"He does not have to *earn* my loyalty, Captain," Remata'Klan said. "He has had it from the moment I was conceived. I am a Jem Hadar. He is a Vorta. It is the order of things."

"Do you really want to give up your life for 'the order of things'?"

Remata'Klan gazed at him with two emotions plying at his eyes, suddenly very human eyes despite the lizardish mask in which they were set. Sisko saw both envy and dignity in those eyes at that moment, and for the first time he found himself involved in respect for a being that had until now been nothing more than a fabricated tool.

As Remata'Klan spoke his final words, he was certainly much more than a simple tool.

"It's not my life to give up," he said with a tincture of pride. "And it never was."

Along with his resolve to do the ugly thing, Sisko also found himself strangely supplanted by noble respect for Remata'Klan's selfless decision. Engineered life-form or not, Remata'Klan had been given as clear and honorable a choice as any soldier could expect—a chance to save his men from certain defeat, and to save all their lives at the same time. The tempting offer, which Sisko would've taken, had been summarily turned down.

Something about that embarrassed him. He knew he would win, but the victory now would be shriveled and flagless.

He made his way back up to O'Brien and the others, fielded a pointless question about what had happened, but he knew the answer showed perfectly well in his demeanor.

The Jem Hadar got back to their pathetic position and opened fire, apparently not wishing to prolong the conflict to which they were committed. Streaks of disruptor energy tore into the rock face, splintering the Starfleet team with shards of mica. Dust blew into blinding clouds. Flying sand blistered their skin.

Sisko leveled his phaser and returned fire. His team took his cue and did so as well, scorching the field below where the Jem Hadar had so little cover. He took out the first soldier himself, seeing with a bizarre relief that it wasn't Remata'Klan.

Like a hologame, they took out the Jem Hadar soldiers one by one, and got a scorching fight in response. Jem Hadar, despite everything, did not die easily—or alone. As Sisko watched from thirty feet away, unable to reach out, Remata'Klan's last shot cut into a fissure and a sheer slab of the rock face slid off the promontory. Even as he admired the Jem Hadar's quick assessment and use of the geology, Sisko choked at the sight of Ensign Paul Gordon's body convulsing in the energy wash of that shot. Before Sisko could cry out for someone to help him or grab him, Gordon tumbled forward to the open air that now lay before him, and followed the slab of rock all the way down to the canyon floor.

The fighting intensity increased. Any hesitation melted away from Sisko, and from his crew. Their arms went stiffer behind the phasers. Their shots were more carefully targeted. In less than thirty seconds, all the Jem Hadar lay dead on the canyon's bottom.

Slowly Sisko rose from the rubble. Pebbles sheeted off his back and crumbled to the slag deck. He led his crew down the jagged escarpment to the canyon floor where Bashir quickly but uselessly checked the still form of Ensign Gordon. At Sisko's signal, Nog and Garak stayed higher, guarding the scene.

With guilt pricking his chest, Sisko knelt at the body of Remata'Klan rather than the body of his own crewman. He knelt there and for a moment wished not to stand again. He felt the eyes of O'Brien and the others, and was strangely irritated when O'Brien spoke.

"Captain . . ."

At first Sisko thought he was being either comforted or mildly scolded, but then instinct kicked in and he glanced up. O'Brien was looking not at Sisko but off at the canyon passage.

Sisko turned and stood. Keevan came slowly through the debris, stepping over the bodies of his soldiers, carrying the communication gear. He paused only once, over the body of Remata'Klan, but the Vorta's expression was unreadable. In fact, he had none.

"You know, Captain," he began, "if I had had just two more vials of white . . . you never would've had a chance."

Loathing chewed at Sisko for this rapacious clown. His jaw tightened. He couldn't speak to Keevan.

"Chief," he said instead, "take him back to base camp and then get to work on the comm system."

"Aye, sir."

"Lieutenant Neeley!"

"Sir!"

"Form a burial detail."

"Aye, sir."

As she turned away, heading for Garak and Nog, Julian Bashir came to Sisko's side, his face heavy with the death of Paul Gordon and the inability of advanced medicine to do a damned thing about it.

"Will we be rescued now, sir?" the doctor asked.

Stiff and sore, Sisko couldn't meet Bashir's eyes. "O'Brien can fine-tune the communication equipment and use it with what we salvaged. I gave him Martok's personal frequency. Might take longer than we'd like, but at least we'll be rescued by someone on our own side. With a little luck, the Jem Hadar in this area won't be able to pick up a frequency that specific. You go back and prepare Dax for transport."

"Aye, sir. . . . What's the matter, Captain? It's over, isn't it? We won, didn't we?"

"Yes, Doctor. Yes . . . we won."

CHAPTER
16

SERENE LIGHTS IN SPACE. In wartime, the harborlights of safe haven were like an old-time cook fire to the hungry mind.

General Martok glanced with satisfaction at the success of his fighter wing and his flagship, which he himself chose to command. *Rotarran* was an old ship, proven and strong, and he preferred it to any other. It was a fine training ship, small enough to handle, simple enough for raw recruits, complex enough to make them into good spacefarers.

Strange thoughts, to be empathizing with those being conquered. Klingons had for centuries conditioned themselves to be the conquerors, to surge forward against all obstacles, even sensations of sympathy for the targets of their overbearance, but now things were different and Martok did nothing more than engage in reverie of Klingon superiority for days. In fact, this was preferable, this alliance with the Federation. He had never resented Starfleet as had so many of his peers. He had, instead, admired them. Generally, the Federation was made up of physically weak races who could not stand one to one against stronger races such as Klingons, but banded together in a common goal, they had been strong indeed and relentless in their purpose. That was to be admired more than physical training. Brains mattered. Only fools believed otherwise, and Martok had never allowed himself to respect the foolish, no matter how fools postured.

Success these days was measured in small increments. The tougher the fight, the smaller the increments. When the enemy was strong and winning, spirits were kept high by small jumps. Today, upon his bridge, he had a small jump for which he and his crew could be proud for a while.

"Are you glad to be home?" he asked, turning to his side and speaking to Benjamin Sisko.

"I'm not home yet, General," Sisko said as he gazed out the main viewscreen at the shimmering lights of Starbase 375. But there was victory in his voice despite the circumstances.

The rescue had come just in time, just before Sisko and his crew starved on that nebular rock, and Martok was pleased to have cast his net and saved them. He and Sisko still had their pact, their purpose, though they had not spoken of it during the voyage back here. Too many risks.

As helmsman, Ch'Targh steered the *Rotarran* into

an approach spacelane, Martok punched his comm. "This is General Martok of the *I.K.S. Rotarran* requesting permission to dock."

"General, you're cleared for docking at Bay Eleven," the station harbormaster responded almost instantly.

Near the rear of the small Klingon bridge, Engineer O'Brien and Dr. Bashir stood together, speaking quietly.

Bashir's quiet breath carried a plaintive, "Thank God. . . ."

"I never thought I'd miss Starfleet field rations," O'Brien murmured back. "Give me some freeze-dried peaches, or powdered carrots, anything as long as it's not moving."

Martok smiled. They didn't think he could hear them. Perhaps they'd forgotton during their time on the wide expanse of rock that a commander on a ship became attuned to any noise on his bridge. They were speaking of Klingon food, of course, and Martok forced his smile to flatten out though he continued to enjoy their squeamishness. Must have been a trial for these humans to come off near-starvation by being treated to Klingon food.

"I don't mind the food," Bashir muttered to O'Brien. "It's the singing."

"Till all hours of the night. . . ."

"If I had to listen to one more ballad about the honored dead, I'd've gone stark raving mad."

"Captain Sisko, Admiral Ross requests that you and your senior staff beam to his conference room for debriefing immediately."

Sisko came to life at Martok's side. "Tell the

admiral we're on our way. General . . . once again, thank you for rescuing us."

Martok turned. "Try not to get too comfortable lounging around that starbase. We need you back in the fight."

He added a little flicker of his remaining eye, indicating that the two of them would speak privately about their own plans at some later date. There was enough to do, there was time to connive.

Sisko offered a smile. "Are you a betting man, General?"

"One of my pleasures."

"Then a barrel of bloodwine says that I'll set foot on *Deep Space Nine* before you do."

"Done!"

Sisko negotiated a good grip of agreement, then turned to shoo his crewmen back to their own lives.

"General Martok, harbormaster."

"Martok."

"Change of plans, General. Your wingship Lach *needs immediate hull plating repair or they'll be down for weeks. If it's clear with you, we'd like to have* Rotarran *orbit the station for a day so we can use that inner slip."*

"We expect new recruits at the starbase. Can you arrange for transport?"

"They're all ready to board the Vor'Nak *and raft up with you in orbit. Then* Vor'Nak *can tranfer Captain Sisko's crew over to the starbase shuttle station. It's some leapfrogging, but it'll get* Lach *back into space sooner."*

"Very well for us, starbase. We shall take orbit."

"Thanks. Stand by for Vor'Nak."

"Standing by. Ch'Targh, you heard."

"Taking orbital attitude, General," Ch'Targh responded gruffly.

"Kich'ta, tell the crew they'll have to wait a day for shoreleave."

"Yes, General. They'll be irritated."

Martok chuckled. "Good. Order my lunch."

In the time it took him to move slowly through his ship to the mess hall, checking on details, speaking to crewmen, dipping into areas to assess damage and encourage repairs, he knew that *Vor'Nak* was docking in the orbit lane. He could hear the subtle crunch of clamps on the outer hull and the gush of the umbilical systems rafting the two ships together according to Starfleet safety regulations, which demanded more exacting care and extra attachments than most Klingon crews bothered to employ. A cold plate of gagh was waiting for him at his table in the mess hall, the delectable life-forms just coming out of their stasis stupor. Barely had he sat down and put his utensil to the fat worms than the door opened and Commander Worf strode in with his usual grouchy demeanor.

"General, I've just received word. The reinforcements from the *Vor'Nak* are here."

"Good. Look at this. Barely moving. I'd give my good eye for a plate of fresh gagh. How many replacements?"

"Five."

Martok looked up. "Five? I requested fifteen."

Worf took the scolding as if this were his own fault. "General Tanas could only send us five."

Pushing his plate away, Martok stood and arched his cramping back muscles. "We keep falling back and the Dominion keeps pushing forward. I tell you, Worf, war is much more fun when you're winning. Defeats make my wounds ache. Ah—replacements."

The door opened again and, in keeping with custom, the new recruits came to the general instead of the other way around. They formed a line and tried to appear appropriate, but Martok and Worf simply gaped at them while sharing a thread of disheartenment. These were warriors?

Two whiskerless youths, two teenaged girls, and a stooped old man. Uch.

Martok sucked back his comments and moved toward them. Worf, the coward, remained behind.

"I am General Martok. Welcome to the *Rotarran*. May you prove worthy of this ship and bring honor to her name."

Dismal. Look at their faces! They're in shock!

"This is a glorious moment in the history of the Empire, a chapter that will be written with your blood. Fight well, and our people will sing your praises for a thousand years. Fail, and there will be no more songs, no more honor, no more Empire. Who among you hears the cry of the warrior calling you to glory?

Clumsily they all raised their fists and shouted "*Qaplá!*"

Well, at least they had been coached.

227

Martok followed the script. "Who offers their life for the Empire?"

In turn, each recruit stepped forward and announced.

"N'Garan! Daughter of Tse'Dek!"

"Katogh, son of Ch'Pok!"

"Koth! Son of Larna!"

"Alexander Rozhenko!"

"Doran, daughter of W'mar!"

From behind, Worf spoke out of place, out of the traditional script. "Alexander . . . ?"

Martok looked at him, then noticed that the boy was returning Worf's glare with frozen eyes.

"Rozhenko?" Martok repeated. "Of what house is Rozhenko?"

"Of no house," the boy said. "My honor will be my own."

Worf stiffened, but said nothing more. Ah, trouble.

"Well," Martok bridged, "there will be much honor for the taking on this ship, enough for all of you. I accept your lives into my hands. Glory to you, and to the Empire!"

With visible effort Worf recovered his composure and barked, "Dismissed!"

The troops filed out. Martok turned.

"This Alexander Rozhenko . . . you know him?"

Worf was staring at the door as it clacked shut, and still he stared at it.

"He is my son."

Martok nodded. It had been easy to suspect. "Such trials are a strain on a small ship. Perhaps you would like a transfer back to Captain Sisko for the time being."

"No, General," Worf said instantly. "My son's coldness will never push me from my duty."

"He will be distracted enough, Worf, and so will you. We have orders at last."

"Orders?"

"Yes. We are to escort a convoy to Donatu Five."

Ordinarily such news would be welcome for idle Klingons, but Martok saw a crimp in Worf's expression and instantly understood. Worf was involved in plans to be married. Also, his child was now on board. Donatu Five—

"The last three convoys sent there were destroyed by the Jem Hadar," Worf uttered, as if remembering. Martok did not believe he was complaining, but the boy *was* here now, and no parent could think that clearly.

"Which is why this one must get through," Martok told him.

With that he succeeded in steering Worf's attention to tactical concerns. "How many ships will form the escort?"

"The *Rotarran* is all the High Council can spare." Martok smiled with anticipation. "A vital mission! Impossible odds and a ruthless enemy! What more could we ask for? I tell you, Worf, I feel young again!" He scooped up the padd that had been sitting next to his listless plate of gagh and handed it to Worf. "Here is the briefing. Start battle drills immediately. Train them hard."

Worf came to life with fresh purpose as his mind

fixed on a concrete task. "By the time we join the convoy, this crew will have the reflexes of a Norpin Falcon."

"I expect nothing less. One moment, Worf." Martok lowered his voice, even though they were alone. "We have shed blood together, escaped a Jem Hadar prison together . . . you have pledged yourself to my house. Yet in all this time, you never mentioned you had a son."

Deeply disturbed, Worf scanned the deck. "It is a difficult subject to discuss."

"That much is obvious."

Worf wanted to leave, Martok knew, but a question had been posed and it would eat at them both until the answers came, one way or another. Rather than let his exec off the hook, Martok stood silent and waited until the air around them began to crackle.

Worf shifted uneasily. "Alexander and I were never close. His mother was only half Klingon and disdainful of our ways."

"I see. You allowed her to raise the boy."

"No, General, she was killed . . . when he was very young. He spent a short time with me aboard the *Enterprise.* After that, I sent him to live with my foster parents on Earth."

"Why?"

"He . . . showed no interest in becoming a warrior. It was difficult, but I learned to accept it and, in time, I encouraged him to follow his own path."

"Then why has he joined the Klingon Defense Forces?"

"I do not know. . . . I have not spoken with him."

So instincts were right—this had been a complete surprise, not just a disagreement or an order disobeyed. Martok raised his stiff arm and placed a hand on Worf's shoulder. "My friend, this is not good. When a father and son do not speak, it means there is trouble between them."

By this, they both knew, Martok was offering to act between the two in some way, to quell the turbulence or take Worf's place as the boy's trainer until things changed. All those offers were endemic in his interference. When ice formed between members of a house serving on the same ship, the result could be clumsiness at best and at worst . . . disaster. As commander, it was Martok's prerogative to push between them.

The response was not really a surprise, though.

"I prefer to handle this in my own way," Worf said.

"Then do so."

And that, they both knew, was an order.

Martok left the mess hall because he knew it would soon be time for the crew to eat and they were uneasy if he ate with them. The unfortunate realities of superior rank. . . .

Instead he went to his quarters, waiting part of an hour until the crew was well entrenched in their meal, then tapped his computer comm unit.

"Computer, where is Alexander Rozhenko?"

"In the mess hall."

"Give me a picture of the mess hall, while keeping the mess hall screens dark."

"Visual of the mess hall on line."

Eavesdropping. An unethical but effective tactic, one of Martok's favorites. Privacy was for women in childbirth.

He sat back, ordered a mug of war nog, then focused his working eye on the smoky room on the screen. The crew was there, crowded to the tables, enshrouded in smoke, drinking, eating, snarling stories to each other and laughing harshly. They had heard the news—a new mission was coming, a fresh chance at glory, a chance to strike again at the claws of the Dominion. Spirits were high.

Then he saw what he wanted . . . Alexander Rozhenko, narrow of shoulder and small of countenance, collecting his meal at the dispersal unit. The boy turned to find a seat, and unfortunately chose one next to Ch'Targh.

Ch'Targh had no children and was intolerant of the children of others.

Equally unfortunate was Alexander's choice of words.

"Is this seat taken?"

How very Earthly a phrase. To an old warrior like Ch'Targh, it would ring of past stresses with humans and the shame of the Empire at having been contained by the Federation for so many decades.

"Alexander Rozhenko," Ch'Targh greeted. "We were holding it just for you."

Martok grunted a laugh and sipped his drink. He wished he could be there.

"I'm honored," the boy responded, like an idiot.

"The honor is ours. Please."

Ch'Targh was actually standing up! As if the boy

deserved the seat! Now the helmsman was pulling the chair out for the boy. Wiping it with his glove. Martok instantly saw the rippling snicker that ran around the table, but apparently the boy saw none of it. Who could make such a show!

Alexander took the chair, fool, and Ch'Targh sat next to him. "Bregit lung," Ch'Targh approved, surveying Alexander's plate. "An excellent choice. Would you care for some grapok sauce?"

The other Klingons had stopped conversing and were watching the sport. If only the boy were stupid enough to refuse—

"No, thank you."

"Oh, you *must* try some. It brings out the flavor." Ch'Targh doused half the bottle onto the boy's plate, until finally the boy grabbed the container.

"That's enough."

"Some bloodwine to wash it down?"

One of the female recruits, sitting on the other side of Alexander, began laughing, and the joke was out. Alexander snapped around to her. "Why are you laughing?"

The girl just shook her head.

Ch'Targh harrassed, "Or perhaps the son of our illustrious first officer would prefer an *Earth* beverage. A glass of 'root beer.' A lump of 'ice cream'!"

The raft of Klingons dissolved into roars of laughter and table pounding.

The boy straightened in his chair. "Are you mocking me?"

Ch'Targh's snaggled teeth showed. "Now why would I mock you, son of Worf?"

"I am called Rozhenko!"

"And I will call you whatever I please!" Ch'Targh's smile dissolved. "And you will learn to like it."

Alexander jumped to his feet, trembling with rage. For someone who had never really been among Klingon's, his self-control was unenviable.

Ch'Targh remained amused. "Does the son of Starfleet's finest think he is too good to eat with us?"

Martok, as he sat there watching, couldn't tell through the screen whether Alexander were piqued at the idea of being Worf's son or of having Worf referred to as 'Starfleet' or at being associated with Starfleet at all. Perhaps all three. Whatever the cause, Alexander's breaking point had arrived. He said, "No . . . have some lung," and dumped his entire plate, sauce and all, into Ch'Targh's face.

Enjoying all this, Martok reeled back with laughter and nearly lost the balance of his chair. Half the contents of his mug splashed down his beard. As he brushed it away, Ch'Targh was also wiping food from his own face and rising to his full height.

Big even for a Klingon, Ch'Targh brushed the two nearest chairs away as easily as he had cast the bregit lung off his chest. "I do not like your smile," he said to Alexander. "Perhaps I will cut you a new one."

Alexander showed his inexperience by drawing his ceremonial dagger. Ridiculous. Ch'Targh drew his own.

Martok chuckled with satisfaction. None of this would have happened if their general had been in the mess hall with them. Now he could watch without impeding the normal flow of events. The secondary blades of Ch'Targh's dagger snapped out for work.

Alexander was quick and small, but Ch'Targh was especially graceful for a large man, even languid in his movements. Any posturing was simply meant to intimidate the boy. Martok recognized the drama. The other Klingons urged them to bloodshed, but no one interfered. Ch'Targh made circles with his blade, but did not attack. This was too much for the boy, who finally flew forward with a clumsy thrust. Ch'Targh fluidly sidestepped, forcing the momentum to throw Alexander off balance, then drove his elbow into the side of the boy's face.

Alexander spun like a graviton and splattered to the floor on his ignominious part. The Klingons erupted with joy.

"He fights like a Ferengi," Ch'Targh commented.

In that moment, Alexander came to his feet and nicked Ch'Targh's arm before the veteran could pivot aside.

"Oh, very bad judgment," Martok commented. He should make this a training tape.

"Shakk-Tah!" Ch'Targh swore. A big Klingon, yes, but Ch'Targh had a low tolerance for pain.

"And bad timing," Martok mentioned as he saw Worf enter the mess hall. From this vantage point, he was the only person who saw Worf come in. Even those in the room hadn't noticed.

Worf stood as if in shock, peering through the shouts and waves, searching for the cause of this chaos. Perhaps Worf had not yet seen that his son—

Alexander attempted another swipe at his tormentor, but Ch'Targh avoided it again and smashed the heel of his free hand into the boy's face, driving him back into the nearest wall, dazing him like a stricken sparrow and leaving the boy's face bleeding freely.

"Your combat training has been sadly neglected, little one." Ch'Targh flipped the blade in his hand. "I will teach you a new lesson. One you will not soon forget."

He stepped toward the boy, and Martok imagined the scar Alexander would soon be sporting for the rest of his life, but a strong hand caught Ch'Targh's arm and held him back.

"Mmm . . ." Martok moaned. "Better the scar than this, Worf—"

"Enough!" Worf's judgment was no better than his son's, apparently. Ch'Targh tried to wrench away, but couldn't. Worf backhanded the helmsman with a closed fist and sprawled him over a table. Plates and utensils jangled insanely.

Ch'Targh could do nothing now. Worf was inarguably his superior officer, and strikes by superiors could not be returned.

Worf turned now to his son, but the boy was venomous.

"You had no right to interfere!" Alexander said.

"That's right," Martok commented in the privacy of his eavesdropping. "Good boy."

"You will both report to the medical ward immediately," Worf barked. "After they have finished with you, you will remain in quarters until your next watch."

Alexander scowled and put his blade in its dagger, then stalked away from his father.

Worf swung to the other Klingons. "The rest of you, back to your stations now!"

"They'll resent that," Martok muttered. "Worf, we must adjust your people skills."

Grumbling, the other warriors shuffled out of the mess hall. Ch'Targh rolled off the table, now wearing most of everyone else's dinners, retrieved his weapon, and paused before Worf.

"Are you going to fight the Jem Hadar for him as well?"

"Mmm," Martok grumbled around a sip. "Quite right. Computer off. Martok to bridge."

"Bridge."

"Disengage from the Vor'Nak immediately. Inform the harbormaster we will take on supplies out here in orbit, then depart immediately for the Donatu Sector. I am tired of waiting and I think the crew is also."

"Yes, general."

"And tell Worf to begin training exercises. Our first officer needs to concentrate."

Four days into the transit to Donatu, Martok called Worf to his quarters on the bluff of reviewing the training log. That, of course, meant that he was obliged to actually look at the log for a few minutes and make a comment.

As Worf stood before his desk, Martok studiously scanned the information, name after name, response after response, and pretended to be interested.

"The response times are much better. Keep working them. Sit down."

Uneasily, Worf took the chair as ordered. Martok poured Worf a nog and one for himself. "Two more days until we reach the Donatu System. We should be hearing from the Jem Hadar soon."

"Yes."

"There's only one thing I hate about convoy duty. The waiting. After all these years, you'd think I'd be used to it. But nothing is better for breaking tension than a tankard of war nog. Except . . . maybe a good brawl."

That comment set Worf into a glare. "You heard about the fight in the mess hall. . . ."

Martok looked up from a good long slug of drink. "But not from my first officer. I lost him the moment his son stepped aboard this ship."

Worf set his mug down. "You think I acted improperly?"

"It is not easy to stand aside and watch someone injure your son," Martok offered, and managed to soothe some of the crispness from Worf's expression.

"Alexander was no match for Ch'Targh," the first officer said. "He would have killed the boy."

"Ch'Targh might've cut him a little, maybe broken a few bones, but nothing more. You say Alexander never wanted to become a warrior . . . clearly he has changed his mind. You are his first officer, Worf . . . teach him to survive! The Jem Hadar will not be as forgiving as Ch'Targh."

Only a moment later, Martok would have offered

to train Alexander himself, for this might be more effective. Then at least the boy would not be first fighting to climb the mountain of his resentments for his father. But the ship's general alarm interrupted his thoughts. From the bridge, the comm unit bellowed.

"Battlestations! Alert status one!"

"Report."

Martok clumped onto the bridge. Behind him, Worf stormed along as they both landed on the command deck.

Ch'Targh was at his helm. At the sensor array to Martok's left was the boy Alexander. N'Garan, the new female recruit manned the engineering and long-range sensors.

Trial by fire. Good enough. Better than squabbling in the mess hall.

"Jem Hadar attack ship bearing one-seven-zero mark zero-four-five," the boy reported nervously. "Estimate weapons range in twenty-two seconds."

Dumping into the command chair, Martok ignored Worf at his side. "On screen."

The viewscreen flickered to show a wide expanse of empty space. Empty?

Had the boy read his sensors wrong?

"Where is it?"

"I have no target on my sensors," N'Garan said, trying to cover her unease with volume.

Worf glared at the screen. "Reroute primary sensors to weapons controls."

"Aye, sir," his son dutifully responded, and Martok was pleased by that. The boy was not so immature as to let his personal irritations keep him stony while at work. "The Jem Hadar has launched two torpedoes."

Worf looked at him. "At us or at the convoy?"

"At us, sir. Impact, ten seconds!"

"Drop cloak," Martok snapped. "Raise shields. Evasive action!"

Frantically the crew complied. The ship lurched as inertial dampers struggled to catch up with the sudden radical change in course.

There was a tremor in Alexander Rozhenko's voice. "Torpedoes still locked onto us. They will hit in four seconds. Three—"

The arms of the chair were hard and cold under Martok's hands. "Brace for impact."

"Two—one!"

Tense, the crew hunched for the strike. Two seconds . . . three . . . four . . .

"Reinitialize primary sensors," Worf ordered when nothing happened after five seconds.

"Sensors reinitialized," Alexander quickly responded. "The—the Jem Hadar ship is gone!"

"Of course it is gone," his father growled. "You forgot to erase the battle simulation program from the sensor display!"

All heads turned toward Alexander. The boy stared in devastation at his control board, his shoulders hunched in horror of embarrassment.

Exasperated, Martok heaved an audible sigh.

"Stand down from alert status. Resume course. Reactivate cloak."

Only more irritating than the stupid mistake was Ch'Targh's grin as the helmsman stood up, moved to Alexander's side, and sat down there. "Keep a close watch. There may be more hostile simulation programs out there."

Ch'Targh dropped a rough hand on Alexander's shoulder and laughed unremittingly.

Martok watched without interference. When a shadow passed over his good eye, he launched his gauntletted hand and stopped Worf from crossing in front of him. "Wait," he ordered quietly. "He will never make that mistake again. And it's better for us to be too ready than not ready enough."

The rest of the crew was laughing now, covering both Worf's move forward and Martok's halting him. Ch'Targh gripped Alexander's shoulder and shook him. "At least you're keeping us on our toes."

And Martok found reason now to laugh also, and there was something about the laughter that communicated belonging to Alexander rather than resistance, for the boy began to sheepishly smile.

Martok kept his voice low, between himself and Worf. "You see? They have accepted him."

Grimly Worf relaxed a little. "They have accepted him as the ship's fool."

"Mmm," Martok grunted. "Come with me."

Hoping not to make their departure too obvious, Martok circled the long way around the bridge, peeking at some readouts here and there, making the new recruits nervous, and finally led the way around to his ready room door. He clomped inside, and Worf slipped in silently behind him.

The door slid shut.

"Have you spoken to your son about the wedding plans you have?"

Staring down the barrels of the two biggest concerns in his life that didn't involve the war, Worf visibly hardened, then almost immediately let the hardness dissolve. "A father has no need to consult a son regarding wedding plans. The house structure of Klingon family goes from parents to child, not the other way around."

Martok dropped into the chair behind his desk. "My friend, you make your own troubles."

Worf sank into the other chair and then somehow continued to sink further. "I . . . have so little ability to make relationships go smoothly. . . . I find myself fortunate to have found a woman who fits so well into so many cultures."

"Yes, and who is three hundred years old but still appears to be young."

"She *is* young!"

"Yes, of course, and why are you shouting?"

"I do not know."

"Well, I do." Martok attempted to sag a bit in his own chair so Worf would not feel so small. "Marry your woman and train your son. Embrace them both as part of your private world. Let them know they are part of each other through you. Pull down the fences between you. A wedding is just a wedding, Worf, not a state occasion. You fret too much about details. You embrace tradition frantically, but you forget why we have traditions. Not for the sake of having tradition, certainly. Even if all tradition is thrown into the warp core, when all is over, you will be married and Jadzia will be one of my house. And your son, if he wishes, will be one of my house too. He will grow up, Worf. He will change. Time works on a young man. You want him to change in the next ten minutes. Forget that! You did not grow up in a day. *I* did not grow up in a day. Why do you expect your son to come here and grow up today?"

Worf glared at him for several seconds. "Is that what I do?"

Martok leaned forward with his elbows on his desk. "My friend, you are a manufactured Klingon. You were raised by humans who tried to give you an idea of being Klingon, but it was a *human* idea of what Klingons are. They tried, I never deny that they tried, but they were still humans looking inward from afar. This is why you struggle and why you cling to details of tradition too much. There is no mold for behavior that comes in a bottle and has 'Klingon' stamped upon the label and which will sour if not refrigerated. Alexander was raised the same way. Among humans, with a sense of unbidden guilt that he is not Klingon enough. Perhaps it's not you he resents, but being too much like you. I don't know . . . I am no ship's counselor. You think he resents you?"

"Yes. He told me so."

"He lies."

"Lies?"

"Yes. He lies to himself."

Worf looked quite disturbed. Even hurt. "Why would you say this to me?"

"To destroy and diminish you and give Ch'Targh your job." Martok fixed a responding glare on him, then scolded him further with a thump of his flat hand on the table. "Worf! Wake up! Alexander tells himself he resents you. Then he tells it to you, so he gets an upper hand for a while. Every teenager does such things, man. Every young hawk going from the nest first wants to fly around the nest and defy those who built it."

"I do not understand that. . . ."

"Do you not? Well, further be confused by this— your son was assigned to the *Tur'Nask*. He requested transfer. He was given transfer to the *Gurshk*. He again requested transfer. He was finally assigned to *Rotarran*."

Fuming over this news, even Worf seemed to be warmed by it. He gazed at the desktop. "He should be transferred . . . then he could concentrate on his work. Any work other than being my son, or *not* being my son."

"If it comes to that," Martok agreed, "he will be transferred. But we shall make any tranfer temporary."

Worf looked up. "Temporary?"

"Of course. Father and son should ship together eventually, but after each is secure in his purpose. Oh, we will somehow fail to tell Alexander that the transfer is temporary. Are we clever? Or cowards? I don't know. We'll send him to another ship to become a real crewman, if that suggests itself as the best way. For a while, he can stay here and we shall see. Despite the harrassment he receives in your shadow, I have received no request for transfer from Alexander, and that tells me a great deal, Worf. The young hawk circles you. For now be proud, and show him the way to fly."

Let us have faith that right makes might, and in that faith let us to the end dare to do our duty as we understand it.

Abraham Lincoln

CHAPTER
17

The *Defiant* has been operating out of Starbase 375, conducting forays into Dominion controlled space. While the missions have taken a toll on my people, they remain determined to do whatever it takes to win this war. As do I. One thing that's made all this easier, if not more of a balancing act, is that Charlie Reynolds of the *Centaur* has been providing backup on some of the missions. For security reasons we haven't filled Charlie in on most of our plans, but he hasn't been asking the wrong questions and that means we can let him in on the action. At least, Ross wants me to consider Charlie an asset, and even though I resisted at first, it does seem to be working out.

I guess it's good—it gives my crew the idea

that they're not so alone. Charlie Reynolds is now one of very few captains who have any idea at all that Starfleet is working on covert actions. He doesn't really know what I'm up to, but I can tell from his sarcastic evil eye that he's always thinking and adding things up that nobody in his right mind would add up.

I wish we could tell everyone, all the people we really do trust—maybe then I wouldn't feel so alone either.

My meetings with Martok have been very rare because we have to be tightly secure, but they've been fruitful. He has been involved with recruiting more Klingons for our cause and training younger warriors for active duty. Not a job I envy him, and certainly not with Mr. Worf on board the *Rotarran*. Worf will expect those young Klingons to accept some version of Starfleet regulation in order to work as our allies. It must be quite a show going on over there. Worf has been tight-lipped about whatever they're doing, but I can tell he isn't happy. A shipload of recruits and an unhappy Worf . . . Martok's got his hands full.

The general just finished secretly charting all the stations in that sensor array in the Argolis area and funneling that information through Starfleet Intelligence to Admiral Ross. Now we can make a plan for assault. Frederick the Great said, "He who tries to defend everything defends nothing." That's my goal—to blind the Dominion so they can't track the movements of Starfleet squadrons. That way, they'll have to defend everything. Their forces will be spread thin. That's when we move in a major assault.

I have to play my cards carefully from now on. Commanding a battleship on special maneuvers and also juggling an advisory desk job for Ross has been tricky. Even more difficult has been keeping Ross from noticing that it's tricky. I have to be valuable enough to him to keep my inside position, but not so valuable that he wants me here full-time. I admit to feeling torn—they do need experienced advisors at Starfleet Command. I just don't want to be one of them.

THE MESS HALL aboard *Defiant* was crowded with scruffy but victorious officers and crew. They'd just docked after returning from another covert and hazardous mission—another successful one. With careful planning on many fronts, the alliance was starting to take nips at the Dominion. Judging from the fierceness of the responses, the nips were starting to sting. Slowly but surely, the effort was starting to come together.

Over there, Nog had set up a makeshift bar, complete with bottles and glassware, and was playing Quark's role for the crew. Sisko approached the bar with Dax and Bashir, knowing they were all showing signs of fatigue along with the satisfaction. The *Defiant* was under repair—there was always damage— but had proven a tough-hulled ship with flexible systems and had so far brought them back every time.

They'd been conducting a series of raids on supply and tactical installations, but the trick had been to inflict the raids far enough apart and on a random enough timetable to make them unpredictable, which didn't always fit in with the repairs the ship needed or the rest the crew needed. Several times they'd set out on a mission with only minimal repairs, which compounded the ship's needs and often compromised them. Because the crew had learned to work together so well, Sisko had avoided reassignment of any but the most badly injured of casualties, and that meant recoveries were cut short sometimes too.

Weeks had gone by in the war with the Dominion, and *Defiant* had been almost constantly out on special missions, usually without support. Each time they rested and repaired, but each time there was a little less rest, a little less repair. They never had a chance to recover completely.

So they needed every little bit of encouragement, and today Nog was handing Sisko just enough.

"Saurian brandy? How did you get your hands on this?"

Bashir accepted his glass from the cadet. "In the middle of a war, no less."

"It's a busy starbase," Nog claimed evasively. "I may be a cadet, but I'm still a Ferengi."

Dax raised her glass. "Lucky for us."

"Excuse me, Captain—"

Sisko turned to see O'Brien pushing through the crew toward him, with a large silver tank in his arms.

"Power cell from the phaser array, sir," the engineer said. "We used it up on the last mission."

A used-up power cell—enough phaser energy for a year of conventional service, and it had been used up in one mission. That was how things had gone lately. Sisko took the canister and held it up for all to see.

"Take a good look at this, people! It says something about this ship. It says that we're willing to fight—and that we'll keep on fighting until we can't fight anymore."

Cued by Dax, the crew shouted, "Yes, sir!"

Sisko gazed at the scorched canister. "You don't throw something like this away."

"No, sir!"

He made his way through the crowd as they parted for him, to a place against the wall where a small shelf had been mounted. There, six other canisters from their previous missions stood like sentinels. He set the bottom of the heavy mechanism in place, then let its nose bump against the wall.

As he turned, the crew broke out into cheers and applause, until Nog's voice piped over the noise.

"Admiral on deck!"

"As you were," Admiral Ross allowed quickly enough that their fanfare and good spirits weren't snuffed.

The crew fell noticeably quieter, but were still too pleased with themselves to quiet down completely, admiral or not.

"Ben," Ross greeted, moving immediately to Sisko. He was carrying a padd, but didn't mention it or hand it over.

"Admiral."

"Let's take a walk."

"Corridor?"

"Yes, good."

"What was going on in there?" Ross asked as the mess hall door closed behind them and cut off the noise of the crew.

"Just a little ritual we fell into," Sisko said. "It helps the crew unwind."

"They deserve it. They've done a hell of a job."

"Thank you, sir. But you didn't come here to tell me that, did you?"

Ross smiled, but there wasn't much underlying joy. "No, I didn't. Ever since this war began, the Dominion's been able to outmaneuver us at every turn. No matter where we send out ships, they always seem to be there waiting for us."

I know. It's because they're watching our every move.

"I've noticed that," Sisko said, without tipping his hand.

"It's almost enough to make you think they're smarter than we are, but they're not. They've just had an edge we didn't know about until yesterday. Star-fleet Intelligence located a massive sensor array hidden on the periphery of the Argolis Cluster. The damned thing can monitor ship movements across five sectors."

Sisko controlled his expression. "That's how they've managed to stay one step ahead of us."

Ross nodded. "They've had an enormous tactical advantage. I want you to take it away from them."

"Gladly, sir."

"It's not going to be easy. The array's heavily defended. Here's the Intelligence report. Look it over. I want an attack plan on my desk by oh eight hundred hours."

"You'll have it."

As the admiral walked away, Sisko wondered if he'd

spoken too quickly, given too much away by not asking for a couple more hours. He already knew exactly how he was going to move on the array, and it required another movement by Martok elsewhere to draw the guard ships away from the array, or most of them anyway.

He tapped his combadge. Would this day ever end?

"Sisko to bridge."

"Bridge."

"Locate General Martok on the *Rotarran* and patch me through, private codes and scramble."

"Aye aye, sir."

"This is a kar'takin, a weapon favored by the Jem Hadar. Defend yourself."

The training room was a dark environment, mimicking as closely as possible the confines of a dim and damaged ship. The logic was simple—Jem Hadar ships had limited light, and any allied ship which Jem Hadar had boarded would probably be half wrecked and on emergency lights.

Thus Martok had trouble focusing on the scene being displayed by his personal monitor in his quarters. Better to eavesdrop here than in his ready room or anywhere else—the bulkheads here were soundproof, the door locked, and orders not to disturb him unless an emergency were in effect. So he could quietly interfere upon his turbulent first officer and the turbulent offspring, who would soon be a member of Martok's own house.

Though holding the kar'takin pole, Alexander

snapped into a stance that might be nearly perfect had he been holding a bat'leth instead. Intolerantly Worf lowered his own kar'takin and glowered at his son. Mistakes, mistakes. Worf had the finesse of a nova.

"That is not the proper grip," the first officer spat. "Your thumbs must be opposed so that twisting motions will not—"

"I understand." Alexander jerked the weapon away.

"Then proceed."

As Martok watched, he found himself paying closer attention to Worf's subtleties of temper than Alexander's movements of defense and offense. Those would come around with age, size, and experience, but Worf's truncated mental methods bore tending. If Worf failed to rein his personal troubles, he would soon be ineffective as a dependable first officer. Any officer with a child on board had divided considerations. That was a fact of shipboard life.

Alexander circled his father now and Martok watched with mild interest at the uninventiveness of the young mind. Worf held his position and tracked his opponent, but Alexander seemed not to know what to do. So Worf struck first. Alexander swept his weapon up respectably enough and met the blow with a resounding CLANG that made Martok wince with annoyance as the comm system enhanced the sound it did not recognize. That should be fixed. Who was the duty engineer this morning?

"No!" Worf shouted. "Do not try to shove my blade away! Deflect it and use your momentum to counter."

"I know!" the boy foolishly argued. If he knew, then—

"Then do it!"

Worf swung the weapon again, deliberately leading his student, but Alexander instinctively blocked the blow exactly as he had before and this time was jarred dangerously off balance. A death blow would've followed that, under the dictates of real combat.

"Don't try to fight force with force," Worf said, engulfed in his own battle for reasonableness. "You will lose every time."

Again they swung, and again Alexander failed. The weapons went flying and clattered to the floor. Martok shook his head. No, it was not the boy who was failing.

"What did I tell you?" Worf shuddered with rage. "Pick it up! If you had kept practicing what I taught you when you were a boy—"

Alexander picked up his weapons and whirled on his father without warning, and without listening to the end of the lecture. A fury of wild swipes and thrusts flew at Worf, who easily blocked and parried them, but a pattern of shock was rising on Worf's face. Martok leaned forward and watched with great interest. The boy's fanatic hostility was disturbing. He was flailing at Worf not with experience or determination, but with raw disdain. Soon Worf hooked the weapon with his own and it went flying again.

"What's wrong with you?" Worf demanded at the pause.

Alexander tossed his weapon to the deck. "I knew it would be like this."

Worf lowered his own. "Like what?"

"You must be pleased," the boy said with a belligerent step forward. "Now you can tell me what a failure I am as a Klingon."

"Alexander . . ."

"Or are you just going to send me away again?"

Ah. Martok tilted his head and listened for clues. That was one—being sent away.

Seeming bewildered by words that gave Martok such insight, Worf tried to revert to his mentor role again—the irretrievable role.

"We are not playing in holosuites now. This is war. The Jem Hadar will cut you to pieces."

"Then I will be dead," Alexander defied, "and you will be happy. Now leave me alone."

A guttural chuckle rose in Martok's throat. Such typical resistance. The wild imaginings and carryings too far of a teenage mind. The spouting of statements that were perfectly ridiculous and everyone knew it. Even Worf knew it, for he made no reaction to the spouting. The significance of Alexander's declaration had nothing to do with the message of the words.

Martok chuckled again. Worf appeared so deflated and confused. Worf had never raised children. Martok had raised seven. Some were warriors, some were not. Some were better at other things. If everyone was a warrior, who would do the other things?

What was to be done now?

Wait a few hours. Then do what every good commander does best. Butt in.

Alexander Rozhenko looked exhausted as Martok slipped into the training room. The boy was in the middle of the mats, moving through a training exercise with his bat'leth, the crescent-shaped blade flickering in the simulated evening light. His movements were clumsy, his limbs sluggish, and when he noticed Martok standing there watching him, he began the series of movements again but without any better skill. In fact, tension gripped the boy and his bat'leth slid right out of his hands, slapped to the deck, and barely missed a surgical maneuver on Alexander's foot.

Martok stooped, picked up the weapon, and naturally balanced it in his left hand.

"Fine blade," he muttered. "Well balanced. But in the end, it is only as good as the warrior who wields it."

Then, internally, he laughed at himself. Cliches! Stating the obvious. The harbor of a bored and grumbling grandfather who wished he were a father again. Hah! That was funny too.

"I need more practice," Alexander muttered, struggling between meeting his general's eyes and not daring to meet them.

"Rest a moment," Martok told him reasonably. "You look like you can use it. Tell me, Alexander Rozhenko . . . why are you on my ship?"

The boy drew himself up straight. "To serve the Empire, General."

Disgusting. Martok set the bat'leth back on the weapons rack. "That is a slogan, not an answer. Say what is in your heart."

Perhaps the evenness of Martok's voice made the boy uneasy. No—he was already uneasy. But certainly Alexander, raised among humans, was used to the image of a Klingon grunting and roaring and barking and generally bulldozing his way through life. He felt the natural surges of adrenaline to which Klingons were more succeptible, but his human restraint made him balk when he found a restrained Klingon. Martok's quiet words seemed to both calm and confuse the boy. But why should every sentence be spat like venom? What a waste of energy.

Alexander twitched and shifted. "Do you question every new crewman this way?"

Feigning anger, Martok approached him. "I have no need to. I look in their faces and I know why they're here. They are Klingon warriors. They have answered the call of Kahless."

"So have I!"

"Lie to yourself if you must, but not to me. You do not hear the warrior's call. So I ask again . . . why are you here?"

Shuddering now, Alexander lowered his eyes. "I'd rather not say."

"What?"

"It's a . . . private matter."

"You are as tight-lipped as your father."

"I am nothing like him!"

Allowing himself to explode—perhaps behaving stereotypically would actually relax the boy—Martok roared, "You are both stubborn, tiresome Qu'vatlh! The only difference is . . ." And he grew abruptly calm again. ". . . I need him. But I don't need you."

Anxiously Alexander tensed and stepped forward. "All I ask is a chance to prove myself—"

"I just gave you one. And you failed. You father has requested that you be transferred off this ship."

The boy flared. "He had no right!"

"He has every right. Both as your superior officer and as your father. At twenty-three seventeen, you will transport to the cargo vessel *Par'tok*. Collect your gear. Now."

A good lie was as powerful as any blow. When twenty-three seventeen arrived, Martok knew, there would be no *Par'tok* in the area and some story would be contrived about how the cargo ship was detained or boarded, captured, something. Meanwhile, the boy would either sulk, and thereby give away his inner lack of resolve, or he would take action with his father that would lead to a final eruption of the swelling wound between the two.

And about time.

Worf sat in the mess hall, alone. It was ship's night. No one would be here for hours. That was good, for he was surly. Alexander's presence on this ship had been a constant irritation. Even the crewmen were treating him differently, watching him for reactions, wondering how they should handle the first officer's son. In some faces he even saw the ugly spectre of ambition. If this tension drove him to distraction, he would be unfit as first officer and someone else would move into his place.

He had tried to think of what should be done, but answers evaded him. He wished he were back on *Deep Space Nine*, in the command of Ben Sisko and simply exacting orders to keep an enemy at bay. This clumsy new aggression to try defending a whole quadrant was undirected and troublesome. Goals were opaque, successes tempered. The right thing to do remained cloudy and evasive. Like being a parent. What was best?

He knew he was a miserable excuse for a father. That was why he had sent Alexander away, and now Alexander despised him for doing what Worf had thought was best. Is it not best for a child to be away from an inadequate parent? Not best to have the full-time attention of two adults, not the partial attention of one adult who has no inclination to raise a child?

Yes—yes, that had been right! Alexander *had* been better off with the Rozhenko's than tagging behind Worf on a ship where children should never have been living. It had been right. He would do it again. He would happily do it now, and send Alexander to another ship, where the boy could learn what a spacefarer needed to know without thinking all the time that his father was on board. A captain and officers were what young spacefarers needed. Not parents.

Before him his rokeg pie was untouched. He had ordered it with all the intention of eating, but now that the dish sat in front of him, glowing and quickly cooling, he had no appetite.

This was foolish. To let a child upset him to stultification. And that was something to consider— was Alexander's presence indeed curtailing Worf's own efficiency? That could never do for long.

And he knew it was true. He was failing as a father, an art at which he was inexperienced and untrained, but there was pitiful little excuse to fail at being an officer, a job for which he was qualified and long-tempered. He would never tolerate such troublement in anyone else—

A Klingon dagger lanced through his ruminations and detonated his thoughts. The blade rang upon the table and bit a good three inches into the tabletop beside his plate. The rokeg pie erupted from the vibration and bled all over its crust.

Alexander glared down at him. Worf stood up sharply.

"You are fortunate that I am your father," he said. "If you had challenged anyone else in this manner you would be dead right now."

"If you want me off this ship," Alexander returned, "you're going to have to kill me."

"Do not tempt me." Irritated, Worf put a pace between them. "I do not want to hurt you, Alexander. I want to help you."

"By getting rid of me? All you've ever done my whole life is send me away!"

"I am a Klingon warrior," Worf told him. "I lead a warrior's life. That is not the path for you. You told me that yourself. And I have come to accept it."

"How! By ignoring me? You call yourself my father, but you haven't tried to see me or talk to me in five years!"

The truth of that bolted through Worf's chest. Sending the boy away for his own good—that could be excused. Not contacting him . . . no, there was no excuse. He had never faced the repercussions of his own silence.

"I wasn't the kind of son you wanted," the boy said, "so you pretended you had no son. You never accepted me. You abandoned me."

Worf digested the boy's inarguable point of view—of course he would see things that way, and if honesty were religion Worf would have to ask forgiveness for his abandonment not of responsibility, but of spirit.

Perhaps there was something to proximity.

His son's words stung and stung, until his ears rang and he could hear the strident jangle of his frustrations and his failings and wondered if the damage would always scream like this.

"Battlestations. Alert status one."

Worf shook his head to clear out the scream, but it continued. Martok's voice—they were under attack! The jangle was the ship's general alarm!

"Battlestations. Commander Worf to the bridge. All hands to battlestations."

The glaring paste of familial tension sheared away and suddenly Worf and Alexander were crewmates with a common goal—get to the bridge, take posts, defend the ship, defend the Empire and the Federation, for each was a child of either.

Before they reached the bridge, the bird-of-prey took several hard hits—the enemy must've sprung upon them from some hiding place or a very good cloaking mechanism, for the shots were direct, not at angles, and bluntly striking the hull. Vibrations of return fire whined through *Rotarran*'s hull, as audible as the alarms, savaging whoever was attacking them.

When Worf stormed the bridge with Alexander behind him, General Martok gave his first officer the seconds needed to understand that there were two ships after them, not just one. There was already heavy damage creating halos of smoke around the crew's heads. Martok clung to his command chair, waving at the smoke, and glanced at Worf. Worf was looking port, at the engineer who was slumped over his console, his face badly burned, eyes open and unblinking. Other bodies were strewn on the deck. A very bad beginning.

At a second glance from Martok and a quick point of one finger, Alexander slid into the seat where the engineer had been and did his best with the readouts. "Shields at sixty percent."

Martok selected patience—for now. "And the Jem Hadar?"

"Which one, sir?"

"The one shooting at us!"

"His . . . aft shields are down to . . . twenty-five—no, twenty percent and he's losing antiprotons from his starboard nacelle."

"Weapons, lock onto that nacelle."

At the weapons station, recruit N'Garan visibly trembled with adrenaline. "Target locked—"

But before she could fire, *Rotarran* surged upward on another hit.

Alexander's panel plumed into a light show, blowing him out of his chair. As he turned over, stunned, blood pulsed from a gash in his cheek. A good scar someday.

Worf was looking at his son, Martok noticed, but did nothing to help him. Shaking and dazed, Alexander pressed his fist to his wound and pulled himself back to his station. The instruments were seared and snapping, hot to the touch, and finally the boy shook his head.

Without making Alexander vocalize that there was nothing he could do there, Martok turned to Ch'Targh and N'Garan in turn. "Come to three-one-seven mark zero-four-five. Weapons, can you hit him?"

"Negative. He's out of range."

Shifting to another station, Alexander pulled the engineer's body away from the console and attempted to read the flickering displays. "We've lost internal communications."

Martok ignored him. That was Worf's problem, and Worf promptly acknowledged his son and stepped to the science station.

"Helm," Martok ordered, "come to course zero-two-zero mark two-two-seven."

"There's plasma venting from the primary impulse injector on deck five," Alexander called past Martok to his father.

Ch'Targh glanced up, then said, "Course laid in."

Martok cranked around. "Worf! Get that plasma leak under control before we lose that entire deck!"

The ship bolted again. That was a belowdecks hit, and that meant casualties. Worf was looking around to see who could go with him, but there were precious few crewmen still standing.

"I can seal the leak."

Who said that? Martok waved at the smoke again. Alexander?

The boy was standing straight, looking at his father, and now at Martok.

"I'm of no use to you here," Alexander admitted. There was no bravado in his voice now—a welcome absence.

Logically, Worf should be the one to go with him, but Martok put out his hard-toed boot and caught Ch'Targh in the thigh. The helmsman looked up, caught his general's glare, and promptly swung around.

"I will go with him," Ch'Targh offered. "It will take at least two of us to secure the injector before it explodes."

Worf glowered at them, and Martok saw the struggle of refusal. But did it make sense that both the first officer and the helmsman should leave the bridge when there was a junior officer here?

No.

Gathering his common sense, Worf acceded, "Go!"

Alexander led the way. Ch'Targh followed. Rather poetic, Martok thought.

Grimly Worf crossed the bridge and took the helm.

"Worf, put us off the Jem Hadar's starboard quarter," Martok ordered, eager to distract his exec. "Weapons, continue to target his damaged nacelle."

Pirouetting furiously through space, gravitons

shrieking in protest, *Rotarran* vectored away from the attacking Jem Hadar and drilled the damaged ship's nacelle, dismembering it neatly until the overload surged into an explosion. And then there were only two.

"MajKkah!" Martok exalted. "Helm! On my command, drop impulse power to one-third and come to course three-five-five mark zero-nine-zero. Weapons, be ready for him to pass in front of us."

"Course laid in," Worf informed.

N'Garan fixed her gaze on her board, valiantly ignoring the main screen. "Weapons standing by."

Martok ticked off the seconds as *Rotarran* decelerated sickeningly, venting plasma that obscured the attacking ship's view and ability to judge distance visually.

"Now!" Martok called.

The deceleration jammed to almost a full stop, pressing everyone forward and making Martok feel as if his arms were being ripped off. On the screen, the pursuing ship shot past them, showing its underbelly. The *Rotarran* pitched on a wing, clearing for fire, and shot full disruptors point-blank at the Jem Hadar.

A moment later there was only the ball of flame that happened when a contained warp core was breached. The *Rotarran* surged backward on the shock wave.

Around him, Martok's surviving crew cheered.

"Well done!" he told them. Yes, it had indeed been well done. Two Jem Hadar gone. A good day.

Without even waiting for the sparkles to dissipate or to survey the deep-fried panels of their bridge as was his job to do, Worf turned away from the main screen. "Permission to leave the bridge?"

"Go," Martok told him. "Stand down from alert status. N'Garan, take the helm." As the damage control team flooded the bridge and Worf departed on the same turbolift, Martok leered at the blooming remnant energy from the ship they had just destroyed. "Go, my friend, and hope your son has not already killed himself."

To be continued . . .

Look for STAR TREK Fiction from Pocket Books

Star Trek®: The Original Series

Star Trek: The Motion Picture • Gene Roddenberry
Star Trek II: The Wrath of Khan • Vonda N. McIntyre
Star Trek III: The Search for Spock • Vonda N. McIntyre
Star Trek IV: The Voyage Home • Vonda N. McIntyre
Star Trek V: The Final Frontier • J. M. Dillard
Star Trek VI: The Undiscovered Country • J. M. Dillard
Star Trek VII: Generations • J. M. Dillard
Enterprise: The First Adventure • Vonda N. McIntyre
Final Frontier • Diane Carey
Strangers from the Sky • Margaret Wander Bonanno
Spock's World • Diane Duane
The Lost Years • J. M. Dillard
Probe • Margaret Wander Bonanno
Prime Directive • Judith and Garfield Reeves-Stevens
Best Destiny • Diane Carey
Shadows on the Sun • Michael Jan Friedman
Sarek • A. C. Crispin
Federation • Judith and Garfield Reeves-Stevens
The Ashes of Eden • William Shatner & Judith and Garfield
    Reeves-Stevens
The Return • William Shatner & Judith and Garfield Reeves-
    Stevens
Star Trek: Starfleet Academy • Diane Carey
Vulcan's Forge • Josepha Sherman and Susan Shwartz
Avenger • William Shatner & Judith and Garfield Reeves-Stevens

#1 *Star Trek: The Motion Picture* • Gene Roddenberry
#2 *The Entropy Effect* • Vonda N. McIntyre
#3 *The Klingon Gambit* • Robert E. Vardeman
#4 *The Covenant of the Crown* • Howard Weinstein
#5 *The Prometheus Design* • Sondra Marshak & Myrna
    Culbreath
#6 *The Abode of Life* • Lee Correy
#7 *Star Trek II: The Wrath of Khan* • Vonda N. McIntyre
#8 *Black Fire* • Sonni Cooper
#9 *Triangle* • Sondra Marshak & Myrna Culbreath
#10 *Web of the Romulans* • M. S. Murdock

Star Trek: The Next Generation®

Star Trek: Deep Space Nine®

Star Trek®: Voyager™

Flashback • Diane Carey
Mosaic • Jeri Taylor

Star Trek®: New Frontier

Star Trek®: Day of Honor

Star Trek®: The Captain's Table

Star Trek®: The Dominion War